THE
TESTAMENT OF
SPENCER

THE
TESTAMENT OF
SPENCER

George MacBeth

216945

ANDRE DEUTSCH

For George Edward Moreton Mann MacBeth
born 4 July 1992

First published in Great Britain in 1992 by
André Deutsch Limited
105–106 Great Russell Street London WC1B 3LJ

Cataloguing-in-publication data
for this title is available from
the British Library

ISBN: 0 233 9 8802 5

Printed in Great Britain by
WBC, Bridgend

Prefatory Note

The setting of this novel is in the future, at the very end of the twentieth century, in an independent and united Ireland. It also has another setting, at a much earlier period, when Ireland was in a sense 'united' – but under English rule: the Ireland of Edmund Spenser, poet, for a time secretary to Lord Gray, the governor, and later Sheriff of the County of Cork.

George MacBeth completed *The Testament of Spencer* just before his final illness. He had lived in Ireland for the last few years of his life. If he had survived and had seen the book through the press, I feel that he would not have thought it necessary to add a prefatory note such as this: he would probably have felt that his Chronology of Edmund Spenser (pages 221–222) gave enough comparative facts to guide the reader through John Spencer's thoughts, actions, and confusions.

However, as editor of the book, and at the risk of stating the obvious, I want to stress that the experiences of John Spencer are in no sense those of George MacBeth, nor are his views. Edmund Spenser was 'real': John Spencer is an invention. The merging of these two is the substance of the novel.

Anthony Thwaite

1

It was a rough crossing, and I was very sick. I came up out of the hold with the headlamps on, and a couple of pantechnicons hard behind, slithering a little on the wide stones as we left the quay. Everything was in darkness and the road was soon empty, the big vehicles falling back as I headed through the streets into the city.

I felt better as I drove, air and warmth clearing my brain as I drove with the window down, and a cold mist running in from the sea. January was never a good month for me, too near my birthday, and there had been high waves. But I felt better in the powerful car.

I squared my shoulders against the leather, and let the speed rise. Then I felt a hand on my arm, and a slight pressure. I lifted my foot from the accelerator.

Turning, I saw your smile, and your head shake, your blue concerned eyes full of worry and love.

'I'm sorry,' I said. 'I wasn't thinking. We'll soon be in the city.'

But we were there already, a shining of foreign gold amongst the dingy squares and the flaring brilliance behind the fanlights. The door of a pub opened suddenly, projecting a lane of light across my bonnet, and in this a man reeled, poised with a violin. Seeing the foreign registration, he lifted his fiddle in the air, then swept his arm round in a gesture of drunken, courteous irony.

Well, it seemed so, anyway. Everything was very bright and significant in the aftermath of sickness, that heightened sensitivity born of exhaustion and recovery. I felt a surge of vomit returning into my throat, and choked it down, as I drove on, and what was for me, back.

There had been soldiers behind the man with the violin, the dark green uniformed figures of the Republic, and I remembered that this was a new Ireland.

There had been soldiers before, but those were English soldiers, with uniforms of a familiar khaki, and their own old-fashioned weapons. This was different.

I found it hard to think of an island without borders or check-points, where there were Catholic soldiers with automatics everywhere, and the guerrillas, when you could find them, were Protestants.

I thought about this, watching two young soldiers at the traffic lights by the old Conan Doyle. The name was changed, but the soldiers were still on their way there for a Guinness. They eyed the car enviously as we moved away on the green, easing the machine pistols on their hips. I felt a twinge of fear, wondering what might happen.

You were saying nothing, but I could feel your eyes on me, and the tension of your uneasiness. You waited with your usual caution, doubtful of interfering before the right moment, and then you spoke, very quietly.

'You all right?' you said.

It was a question. But I didn't answer. The car was moving alongside the wall of a big park now, and it made sense to go faster, and I was letting the engine enjoy its freedom.

Our belts were on, and you didn't mind the speed. The car was on high cruise control, and it was perfectly safe. The computer would brake slowly if anything came within touching distance, animal, vegetable or mineral.

It could be a nuisance on the country roads with branches, but I'd learned when to cut the key in.

The car was fine. You liked the smoothness, and the silence. But the easy movement only served to underline

8

for you my state of mind, what it might be, what might have caused the mood you were bothered by.

'You've gone all quiet. What's the matter?'

'Nothing,' I said, rallying, and smiling at you. 'Really nothing. It's just coming back to Ireland. You know how it is. That, and the tiredness after being sick. But I'm better now. Really I am.'

'It's always difficult remembering,' you said, softly. 'It's the same for me.'

You had turned the fur of your collar up, and were leaning with your head on the car door, away from me. But you weren't reassured.

It wasn't the same for you, whatever we might say. I was thirty years and two wives older, and the distance and time sometimes washed against the shores of our good feelings.

I stopped the car in the town we knew so well, under the shadow of the castle, at a small inn with a yard to one side, and an encircling wall. Before we got out, I reversed the car and parked facing the gate.

When you live with soldiers, you find it hard to avoid the sense of danger. Ever since the war, I'd lived in a world of perpetual threat, and I suppose it pleased me to feel prepared for trouble.

There was a busy crowd at the bar, mostly young, all Irish, and I felt an outsider when I ordered my orange juice, and a Scotch, and a couple of cheese sandwiches. It took me a moment, and a deep breath, to avoid asking for an Irish whiskey, but I knew you didn't like your own country's alcohol.

I came back to the corner where you'd found two stools, laying the drinks down between us, and feeling dizzy when I went back for the sandwiches. I moved between the drinkers with a special politeness I wouldn't have used in England. You have to be careful.

Besides, I'd come back this time wanting to understand

9

the people, anxious not to put a foot wrong. Too much had gone wrong in the past, theirs and mine. I wanted a new start.

'Feel better now?' you said, after a while.

The sandwiches had made a big difference. I was surprised how hungry I'd become, and how tasty the batch bread was, despite the soapy cheese. But I still felt my stomach turn over, watching you drink the raw Bell's.

'Much better,' I said, nodding, then taking your hand in mine. 'Nice to be home. Isn't it?'

Well, it wasn't entirely. Not for me. There was a repeated feeling of uneasiness every time I caught sight of a green soldier, the flash of a sabre, or the gleam of a belt buckle. It didn't obliterate the friendly gaiety, and the natural confidence, of the civilian drinkers, but it went some way to create another dimension, a hint of menace.

'Let's go,' you said, suddenly, rising to your feet. I couldn't think why at first, and then, out of the corner of my eye, I saw a man spitting onto the floor. He had a bad cough, but he was looking directly at me while he spat.

I followed you into the yard, the mist.

'He had a cough,' I began, catching you up. 'He was spitting because of his cough.'

'Yes,' you were saying, while I unlocked the car. 'Perhaps. I expect so.'

You were shivering, huddled into your fake fur, while the rush of air from the heater began. The starter coughed, spat – what other words are there – and two long talons of light sped through the gate from the headlamps and caught a dog on the other side of the road in their beam. It was limping, had only three legs.

Then we were rolling forward, had passed the dog and were out of the Pale – beyond the Pale, we used to say – and into the bottomless darkness of middle Ireland, the great saucer of bog and scrub at the far side of which we would find our new home, a fragment of civilization impaled in the west.

It was there we passed the Ballynoura hills, and I remembered the crumbled ruin, and the knot of ivy in the corner, the way I saw it once long ago. But the night was too dark now, and we were too far away.

'Spenser's castle,' I joked. 'It's in bits already.'

But you shivered, wincing.

'Don't,' you whispered. 'His child died there.'

I felt a shadow go through my guts, the sense of a bad omen.

'I'm sorry,' I said, reaching for you. 'It was just a way of speaking.'

So much language, Liz. There are so many ways of putting things. Even that simple journey becomes an allegory of what we were used to, and what we would have to come to accept. The stockade, the need for bridges, the dog's leg of Ulster, eaten away by the cancers of violence.

Afterwards, there would be plenty of time to think things over, in a lower key. But that first night set the tone we were going to be dogged by. Dogged, yes. Even by our loyal Hengist, with his nose in the wood shavings, looking for prisoners.

For a time, the problems rolled by, one by one. You fell asleep, and then you woke, stirring as if from a dream near one of the small garrison towns, saying

'You know, you went completely green. A pale, translucent green, like poisoned alabaster.'

I laughed.

'I feel completely better now,' I said, meaning this. 'But I wouldn't fancy a brandy.'

'It happened so quickly. You seemed to go out of yourself and come back, like a genie out of a bottle. But then,' you added, more prosaically, 'everyone else was the same.'

11

'Except for you,' I said, admiring your guts. 'You must have the belly of an ox.'

Then I patted this belly of an ox, which would soon bear me our child.

On the near side of Athlone, with an hour to go, I stopped for petrol, twenty pounds worth of it in either tank. The breath from the nostrils of the horses made its own mist in the mist. The same mist, the same weather. Always the same.

But the girl handing me the change was different. She had an Irish voice and a black face.

'More frost, I hear,' she said, then. 'You here on holiday?'

'No,' I said. 'I live here. I've come to live.'

The girl glanced in at your fair hair and your blue eyes. People always thought you were English.

'Welcome to Ireland,' the girl said seriously. 'Good luck to you both.'

So we drove on with a blessing out of Africa, fuel from the Middle East. There was nothing to see of the scattered hamlets, the barren castles, the dozing, fought-over cattle. But this was Ireland, our future home, and all were there, and waiting for us.

The problems rolled by, or receded, but the main problem remained. I had the car on cruise, and was half asleep, letting it do the work for me, when I sensed your face beside me, as if on a monitor. I reached over and touched the tears.

'It's all right,' I said softly. 'It's all right.'

You were in your dream, remembering the past, and how its clammy tentacles could still reach down a telephone, and make me cry.

'It's you I love now,' I said, stroking this precious hair with my hands. 'She can't harm us any more. No-one can.'

But I was wrong.

12

2

I turned the ignition off a little after two. The hands moved and paused in the lit square dial of the clock as we sat in the darkness for a moment without speaking. I could hear the wind in the tall spruce where the crows would be roosting, the rain on the metal skin of the car.

'Let's go in,' you said, after a while. But we were both slow to move, not anxious to claim our own.

A light was burning above the door to the scullery, a torch flaring outside the stables. One of the two, or both, it doesn't matter. The haze of light was enough to show the smirr of rain, and a few midges. What there was, I could see.

Where there had once been cobbles, a strip of grass. Shamrock and palms in the beds at the corners. The tall block where the horses had fed, and then the priests and the old people. The torn-open Palladian shape of the wood-shed, a *trompe-l'oeil* in my mind, a folly in the Italian style, but now a row of broken windows and a door clapping on rats.

'Let's go in,' you repeated, more softly, interrupting the shift of my eyes across the yard, and I nodded, and smiled. You won't have seen in the dark, but it pays to smile. There are times when the muscles need exercise.

Then I was turning the rusty key in the big double doors, aware of you shivering beside me, dancing and rubbing your knees together, a beautiful skeleton.

'Bloody cold,' I suggested, loving you, and wanting to sound agreeable. But you were already gone, past the

13

boiler and down the short flight of stone stairs into the old kitchen.

I followed at my own pace, looking left for enemies, as a man who carries a sword should always do. But there was no-one there, not even a mangy cat in the servant's hall.

The light was on over the carving table, flooding white on the stone flags and the great arches. Candles had been lit in sconces, yes. The flicker of grease and the smell of stale gravy. A bin spilling rubbish had been strapped for disposal. You get a landlord's eye for minutiae.

We were both very tired, I suppose. I could feel a slight dizziness, looking round the vaulted room in the glare. The sickness had all gone, the nausea, anyway, but there was a sort of after-echo of queasiness.

Then it struck me, like a lift shaft rushing down my throat. We weren't alone. A figure in anorak and wellingtons was standing dead still in front of a log fire at the far end of the room.

'Harland', I said aloud, shocked. Then again, 'Harland,' making it sound, I hoped, more like a greeting. 'I didn't see you.'

But he ignored this, moving aside to let the fire roar in our faces.

'Hello, Liz,' he said, staring at me. 'You don't look well, John. Are you all right?'

I took in his fourteen stone of iron health, small dark eyes and beak nose. Irish to the bone. Blood of the kings, working for the conquerors.

Harland had known the manor man and boy for thirty years. He had come with the stones, and would go, no doubt, when they fell to ruin, long after Liz and I were in the ground.

Well, I was wrong there. But I had the principle right. Harland was the old retainer, as true to the house as a

14

downpipe or a foundation block. As for the owners, we would see.

'The ship,' I said, angry at his perception. 'It was the ship. We had a bad crossing. I'm better now.'

You were warming your hands at the fire, eager for every drop of the blaze.

'Are the cats well?'

One of us, I don't know which. We would both have wanted to know.

'They're well,' he conceded; then, wanting to take things in his own order, 'I've got some tea on the hob.'

He had milk and sugar out, a few dry biscuits on one of our best plates. Copeland, I think, or was it Spanish Gold. He was pouring into a pair of mugs. His own was there I could see already, keeping warm on the stone beside the fire.

'Harland, you think of everything.'

He didn't, of course. You never drink tea. But Harland would soon remember this, too, and make sure he had coffee made. Harland's was a kind of control by kindness, a rule just this side short of interference.

We had had some weeks to learn this already, since we took him on with the house as a caretaker, watching him clear drains and manipulate keys, an invaluable presence. But now he was here for ever. A fixture, and perhaps a burden.

When Dante went down to hell, he had Virgil for a guide. But Virgil decided which of the damned he should see.

We drank our tea, pretending to like it more than we did. We wanted to be on our own, enjoy our house, then get to bed.

'A man was here wanting work,' Harland said. 'He thought you might need a bodyguard.'

Well, it seems funny here. You can tell the tale and laugh over a pint of ale in a cheerful tavern in Shepherd's

15

Bush. But there in Munster, with the wind rattling the bones of dead soldiers in the walls, it didn't sound so out of place.

'He'll come back,' Harland said, lighting a cigarette. 'You can tell him yourself.'

I thought of Riley suddenly, smoking his long dark cigars, tipping the ash on the floors. He had something in common with Harland, the confidence perhaps, and a certain hardness.

'I can get you a maid,' Harland continued, watching Liz. 'She's a good worker. Not like some of them round here.'

There was nothing ingratiating about Harland's condemnations. He spoke his mind, scorning the idle and the dishonest, recommending out of a genuine pride in his knowledge of the best.

You were in awe of him still, but your caution took its decision.

'I'll see,' you said, weary. 'Send her round, then. Harland, I'm tired. I think I'll go to bed. It was lovely tea.'

Harland stared at your full mug, thinking. Then he crushed his cigarette out. I watched his hand shaking, aware with surprise of all that energy held on leash in his nerves. He got up from the bench.

'See you tomorrow,' he said, reluctantly perhaps.

'Good night, Harland,' I said, walking up the stairs with him to the door. 'Thanks for staying so late. There was no need.'

There were a couple of saddles on the pommel of the balustrade, and Harland stood leaning on these for a moment, looking out through the arch across the yard. Rain falling, pools of light and haze. Gates on three sides, but a good field of fire.

'It's best to keep an eye on things,' Harland said. 'You never know.'

16

Then he was gone, towards his home and his horses, and there were only the cries of bullocks in the night.

I went back downstairs, feeling tired and strange. You were resting with your head on the table, half-asleep.

'God, he's a worker,' I said, laying another log in the grate, watching the sparks falling as white ash.

'Bloody nuisance.'

'Yes, well he could be. But he's loyal.'

'I hope so,' you said, then, 'Stroke the baby.'

So I went round the table, and sat beside you, and put my arms round my son in his cradle of flesh and bone. Daughter and heir, whatever. You were still like a willow wand except where the dome rose in your middle, the omphalos, the place of being. Slender and beautiful.

'Am I really?' you asked. 'Slender and beautiful. Say it again.'

Sweet Thames run softly. Later, we mounted the stone spiral hand in hand, where Harland had placed vases of holly and ivy in all the arrow-slits. By the light only of the plough we crossed through herbs and rushes to our four-poster.

I lay for a long time afterwards, while you slept in the crook of my arm. Then I laid your hair gently on the pillow, and felt you turn, murmuring contentedly.

I was too alert to sleep, and I rose and sat in the wide window, looking south towards the hill of slaughter beyond the farms. An English army had been defeated here. Not far away were the ruins of an abbey, built as a penance and in thanks for victory.

Nothing changes, I thought. They accept us, and then they murder us in our beds. But they need our help, whatever they say. Civility has the face of the Queen.

Idly, I turned the pages of a newspaper on a table beside me. The economy was in trouble. There was talk of bringing the rates back. A priest had been stabbed and killed in his house by a man on the run.

You were sleeping, calm and at ease. I watched you, vaguely uneasy. Then, determined to settle in before I slept, I went down the stone spiral again and out through the double doors.

I unlocked the boot, and began to unpack the suitcases. Overhead, the first hints of dawn were coming, but it was too dark to see, too wet and too far away.

I felt a pressure against my calves, and looked down, sensing the cats almost before I knew what they were.

'Black Prince,' I said, lifting my heavy favourite in my arms.

She was all squirming and velvet, a woman with the name of a great male warrior. But I was never good on sex.

I put the cat down, and carried my baggage into the house, the landlord of a trembling estate. What must grow here could flower in language, as never before. Words began to bud as I unlocked your clothes, as I carried my books to their proper stations.

It was after five when I finally lay down beside you.

3

The day after we landed, I woke to snow. I went over to the window, picked up my watch, and saw it was noon. The sun shone straight down on a scatter of white across the fields, light snow and already melting. But the lake had frozen, and it was only discernible as a black ring and an arc of trees.

You were downstairs, cooking, warm in your blue ski-suit. I found you – kissed you, I remember – then had my bath in peace. Condensation ran down the walls, but this was a place of plastered ceilings and great halls. I could breathe in the grandeur of the vanished masters as I soaped my knees.

Yes, or broke the ice. Waded into the bottomless water, and remembered the drowned soldiers, the banker's body that still blocked the well. This was one of the many legends about the house I'd been told when I put the money down in the dry solicitor's office, earning that yellowing scroll with the Queen's seal, becoming the owner.

'The man who built your house put in a window for every day of the year,' the old secretary with a pince-nez told me. 'He ran a farmer's bank, but he had his aspirations. Your house was a honey-trap for a grand suitor. His daughter paraded through those long rooms like a Queen Bee, until she found her baron, and left.

'Married, and died. The same as her father. The farmers came one dark night and asked for their money, found he had none. He'd spent it all, cavorting in Dublin. So they broke his carriage wheels, dropped his body down the shaft into the water.

'It's poison since. That's why you drink the spring.'

Loquacious, like all the Irish, but I believed her. You have to believe the magic, to write poems. What I wanted to say, so I thought then, would need every ounce of myth it could get to live on.

After my bath, I dried on a soaking towel. I could hear the sound of rats behind the skirting boards.

The house was full of its tiny rattles and wheezes all down the long back corridor and up the whirling stair. There were sly, winter scuttlings, hints of a waspish hibernation of troubles. But I didn't listen. You have to ignore the worst, in an old house.

I breakfasted in the upstairs kitchen, on soda bread and tangerines.

'Feeling all right?' you asked me, smiling, and I nodded.

I was always all right, when you asked me, even then. You made things all right. The ominous noises dwindled into their own reality, boilers and mice.

I finished with marmalade and went into the library, feeling the white light from the snow sleeting in over the boxes. It was a high, echoing room, with bare floor boards and all the packed books waiting to be set free. A thousand volumes bound in leather, the property of a gentleman.

I had one of the huge cubes in my hands, ripping the top open, reaching in amongst the stacks, when I realized that Harland was there. It wasn't the low deferential butler's cough. He was always discreet, and there was always this. It was more a disturbance of the air, an electrical current announcing presence.

You felt Harland more than saw him, or heard him. He seemed to exude a kind of power through intervening space.

'The railings have gone,' he said, with what seemed a

20

cruel satisfaction, as I looked round. 'It was bound to happen, sooner or later.'

He sounded satisfied, but he wasn't, of course. Harland was simply a connoisseur of disaster, and any catastrophe, which confirmed his view of a menacing world, made him feel a right judge of affairs.

'O'Neill was in the pub last night. He was drinking a lot. More than one man heard him say they were going to go.'

Harland was lighting a cigarette, his usual preliminary to a long disquisition. But I wasn't in the mood for this.

'Railings,' I said, straightening my back, noticing slowly what he was talking about. 'You mean the railings beside the main gates?'

'The very same,' said Harland, inhaling smoke.

'Let's go,' I said, leading the way, limping through the hall. We took the drive fast, and Harland in the passenger seat beside me elaborated the bad news.

'The right hand arc has gone, entirely. Sliced through with a laser saw, I'd say. In the night. There's melted iron there, a smell of sulphur.'

'Yes,' I said. 'I'll see for myself, soon enough.'

I was concentrating on missing most of the pot-holes.

'We'll have to get all this re-gravelled,' I said abstractedly, as the car lurched in the pits. Then, focussing on the lost railings. 'Why was O'Neill here? I thought he was up north.'

'He comes and goes,' said Harland. 'He comes and goes, you know.'

Hugh O'Neill had been on the staff of my cousin's department, more than fifteen years ago. He had always had his high connections, but he'd been dismissed for some reason. No-one quite knew why. Disloyalty was the way they always put it.

I don't know, perhaps he had his hand in the till. Anyway, he'd gone, and good riddance to him. But he

21

had a grievance against me, that's for sure. Against the whole boiling of us, I guess, cousins and all.

'It's one country now,' said Harland, reminding me. 'They can come and go as they will.'

We were passing the monument now, with its plaque to the Brownes, mayors and aldermen since before the Flood.

'I know,' I said. 'More's the pity, Harland.'

We sat in silence for a while, digesting this, watching the dull faces of sheep go by, their fleece dirty against the crystals of the snow.

'It's not so much O'Neill,' said Harland, easing his weight in his overalls. 'He's hand in glove with the Desmond brothers.'

It was out now, the real danger.

'Jesus Christ,' I said.

They were all around us, over there in the woods, training their arrowshafts and blunderbusses. They had rectories and bungalows. They were in dispute over half the land in the county. Every acre I owned had been theirs once, and they wanted it back.

'They've always claimed the railings were theirs,' Harland said. 'They say they were never part of the sale.'

By now the car had swung through the stone stanchions, and I came to a halt on the small segment of mown grass at the edge of my land.

I got out slowly. Harland had the shot-gun from under the dashboard, and was covering my back. I suppose. You always took care, at the edge.

I looked left and right. Nothing on the road from Dublin, nothing on the road from Galway. Only a wind, brushing the snow from the tops of bare trees, where there might be leprechauns.

'What a can of worms,' I said.

It was both a waste and a warning. The right arc of the railings had gone, the left arc was still there, a sweep of magnificent iron. Imagine an open mouth, and half the teeth knocked out.

'Itinerants,' I suggested. 'You're sure it wasn't the tinkers?'

Harland shook his head.

'I'm sure,' he said.

I went over and ran my finger along the stone ledge, lifting flecks of metal.

'But why half?' I asked, as of myself. 'It seems senseless.'

Harland smiled, and spat.

'One brother took his half,' he said. 'The other's waiting. That's what I heard.'

The snow began again, and we climbed back in the car, starting the engine for warmth. I started the wipers and watched the holes in my face through the fans. It felt like that, and I shivered.

'Let's go back,' I said, thinking of you. 'I'm afraid for Liz, on her own.'

'She'll be all right,' said Harland. 'They only want to annoy you, make a nuisance of themselves.'

I watched the confetti look of the snow, as we drove back, a marriage of air and cold. Well, it was that all right, the Irish blarney, the English steel.

'It's O'Neill,' I said, thinking. 'He's put them up to this. He's lent them the laser saw, for sure. They'd never have the wit or the irony to think of this on their own.'

Harland was smoking again, the broken shot-gun across his knees.

'He could get them anything,' he agreed. 'He has companies the country over. Any machinery they might need. Swords, guns. He can get the lot.'

'They won't need guns yet a while,' I said firmly, feeling Harland go too far. 'But we'll go to court. I'll sue them for every penny the railings are worth, and a lot more into the bargain.'

23

But I knew I wouldn't. How could I prove it wasn't the travelling people? A bit of drunken talk in a pub, a few flecks of metal on a wall. It wasn't enough.

'Stop the car, John,' said Harland suddenly, and I put my foot on the brakes, expecting a mine or something. I don't know.

He was out on the verge, the mended shot-gun at his shoulder, aiming. Firing both barrels. Then I saw the hare at full speed across a field, rear, bounce.

'Dinner,' Harland smiled. 'I'll go and get it for you.'

Later, parking the car in the yard, I realized that he'd left us defenceless for a few seconds, in the dangerous middle of the forest. There were no more shells.

'Perhaps he had some in his overalls,' you suggested, when I told you. 'Don't be so paranoid.'

But you frowned, I noticed.

Harland helped me unpack my books, and the snow melted, and the railings lingered in my mind, all day.

'It's bad news about O'Neill,' I said, when we ate the hare, moving our forks between the candles. 'I didn't think he'd dare to show his face in the south, even now.'

'The enemy,' you suggested, laying a finger on my lips. 'You're manufacturing perils for your poem.'

Perhaps I was. I don't know. Sometimes it's hard to say.

4

The first time I began to notice what was happening, I went to a doctor. But he wasn't very interested. I remember the waiting room in the basement, and the shelf of theology books. Yes, it was that kind of doctor.

'Move your foot,' he said, looking over his half-spectacles. 'I mean, can you?'

'Of course,' I said, irritated. 'It's not physical.'

But he thought it could be. He went over my whole body with a fine tooth comb, inspected my genitals, took a urine sample.

'No,' he said. 'It's not medical.'

'I know,' I said, even more irritated. 'It's my head. I've tried to explain.'

'Oh,' he said. 'I see. You'd better try a priest.'

Of course, it wasn't as absurd as that. I exaggerated when I told you, making a story out of the funnier parts. But they weren't interested. Neither this doctor nor any of the others.

I can see why. When I went in, I was healthy. All I had was my limp, and my blood pressure, and they weren't a problem. They soon saw that.

'I should take a holiday,' they suggested. 'Write some more of those fine poems of yours. Go back to Ireland. That'll be four hundred guineas.'

They may have been right. I feel fine, most of the time.

'It's the same for all of us,' one of them said. 'We all get muddled sometimes. We all imagine we're someone else,

25

once in a while, old soldiers. Don't worry. You'll pull through.'

So I bought the house. I got married, after all. We both came back to Ireland, where they drank their children's blood, where they ate their own excrement.

They had to, you see. It was our doing.

I went to a priest in Ireland, a dark, furry man with a taste in literature, and a suspicion of women.

'You're on your own, Mr Spencer,' he asserted, eyeing the spare chairs and the doorway to make sure, when I visited him in his frowsty parlour. 'You knew Philip, I imagine,' he began.

We got that out of the way.

'Seamus, too. You must have met Seamus, in your travels.'

But I wasn't there to swap names with him. I took a deep breath, and leaned forwards, into a haze of cheese and onion crisps. Garlic, too. There may have been garlic in his diet.

'The problem is,' I said. Then I drew back, after all it isn't a problem exactly. 'I mean, I sometimes feel that I'm someone else.'

Then it came out in a rush.

'It's not frightening. It's more like a dream starting, in the middle of the day. Or finishing, too. I get bits and pieces, you see. Moments when I feel that I'm not there, that someone else is, that I'm doing things with a different set of people. It's hard to explain.'

The priest was frowning, making a bush of hair in the middle of his face, eyebrows, moustache and beard all merging into one.

'But it bothers you,' he suggested.

'No,' I said, irritated. 'I told you, it's not frightening. It's even exhilarating, at times. Fun. But I want to work out what's going on. What's happening to me, if anything is.'

A tongue came through the hair on the priest's face, a snake from the grass, licking his lips.

'Are you ever,' he paused. 'Are there women with you sometimes, in these moods?'

'No,' I insisted, hearing his clock on the wall, watching the small frantic lecher. 'Lust is hardly the problem. I have a young and vigorous wife. Naked, sometimes. Even with black stockings on.'

Then I relented. After all, he was trying to help I suppose. Crude as he was.

'I'm sorry,' I said. 'You see, I'm not here for absolution. I mean, I expect that I should be, I'm sure there are sins.'

'There are always sins,' the priest stressed. 'I recommend that you clear your mind, then come and see me again.'

I remember the tasteless plaster Virgin on top of his book-case, the incongruous dinky toys, an impermeable sense of innocence and appalled concrete bigotry.

'I'm not a Catholic,' I pleaded. 'It's trying to clear my mind that's the problem.'

Later I asked my solicitor. We had some deeds out in his office, or it may have been a consultation about the railings. I don't remember.

'Sean,' I said. 'Let me ask you something. Are you ever worried you might be somewhere else? I mean, when you're here at your desk, under your hunting prints, doing your business, worried it might be your grandfather or someone who's there with the quill in his hand, signing a will?'

'I'm not a drinking man,' he said. 'You know I touch very little during the day. No more than a half of Murphy's.'

Then he put down his pen, saw that I was serious.

'John,' he said, slowly enough. 'We all get a bit dreamy sometimes. Even a dry old stick like myself. I drift away, into the past or the future. Yes, it can happen.'

27

I shook my head.

'It's worse with me, Sean,' I told him. 'Far worse. Or far better, I don't really know which. There are hours on end when I'm taking part in events that don't quite fit with the rest of my life. I'm living the life of a near neighbour, or somebody close to me long ago.'

He was polishing his spectacles.

'I see what you mean, John,' he said. 'I knew a Scots doctor once, name of Macbeth, and he was always afraid he might be a murderer. Because of his name, because of Shakespeare and the play. But he lived a blameless life until the day that he died.'

I laughed.

'Names are a problem,' I told him. 'He must have had more trouble than I have. What bloody man is this, instead of Who's the Fairy Queen, then?'

But Sean was taking me seriously.

'John,' he said. 'I know nothing about this. But surely, you're a writer of books, a poet, a man of imagination. That's all it is.'

'I know,' I said. 'I suppose that's all it is. But it seems more than that, with me. Sometimes, anyway. It doesn't worry me. I mean, I even write about it, once in a while, and then I can't always tell which is the thing itself and which the writing.'

'Must be good then,' he suggested, and we both laughed. Still, I remember one thing he said, when I was about to leave.

I was putting my overcoat on, lifting my brief-case.

'John', he said, rubbing his nose. 'I wouldn't sign those documents until tomorrow, perhaps. You don't seem quite yourself today.'

Beside the embrasure, looking out over water and leaves towards the mountains, I started to wonder. Perhaps a future of wheels would come, wings in the air, red knights running on gravel. The nations locked in combat in the central blue.

It's easy to do that sort of thing, quite consciously. You shake the centuries in the sifter, add a few quotations for good measure, and down it rolls. Burning marl. The vomit of a disordered fancy, tellurian waste.

I don't know when I got the idea for the twelve novels. Twelve or twenty-four, it doesn't matter. I suppose it may have been reading Balzac, the human comedy.

Anyway, it was long before I met you, long before I came back to Ireland, even. I had fragments written in Kent, with Philip. I remember reading more than one whole book to Riley.

So the structure came before the theme. There were always going to be twelve twelves, and then another twelve twelves, if I had the time.

'A man for the gross,' Riley said, only half in jest. 'A dozen merchant, that's what you are, John. Flexible about the produce, but rigid about the number of the boxes.'

'That's what it means to be a classicist,' I told him. 'You have to have glasses, to pour your wine in.'

But it took me a while to find the right kind of glasses, the shape of the prose, the paragraph moving like a stanza.

Then it was easy, life bringing me wine in her own barrels. Anything green, Ireland like a dish of crushable emeralds. The blood-red situations flooding out of history into my hands. A man with a cousin managing the Queen's estate, the secretary at the sharp edge of empire.

You write this, and you know what you mean. You go for a walk in the Earl's Court Road, meet a man in The Grenadier, have a Guinness with him.

'I liked your last one, John,' he says, in the kind heat of the liquor. 'That scene where he tries to wash the blood off his dead baby. Rough stuff, boy. Keep churning them out.'

So you nod and smile, take your meed of praise, and run. It doesn't happen very often, but, when it does, it helps. You can tell the difference between who you are and what you've invented, suddenly. For a few moments only, perhaps, but it keeps you going.

Then I'm upstairs, crouched over these white keys. Watching the silver rings, the steer leaping behind the horseshoe on the back-plate. I bought it for five pounds in an auction, Liz.

It'll see out my time. Three weeks, or three years. Who cares? I can never finish. Too many pages lost in the ruins.

That man in the pub, all he could see was the surface. A good story, that's what he wanted. Some blood and thunder, a bit of spice from me, once a year. Then back home to the wife and the television.

'Tell you who I met today, love. You'll never guess. In The Grenadier, fellow who wrote that paperback about the dead baby. What's his name? You know the one I mean. John somebody. Nice fellow, too. Bought me a pint of Guinness.'

I'm going to bed, Liz. I don't feel well. You get born in London, you die in London. You write your books, they get read by the rich at airports, by the poor in lavatories.

But neither understands. They don't even get the point. They don't even know my books are set in Ireland, they don't remember. As long as there's plenty of killing and screwing, that's all that matters.

But why? Who cares? It's a way of filling in an hour before the news, or the football match, or the flight to Singapore. Makes you shiver, helps you wank. While Philip and Linda and Riley rot in their graves. Or will. While all that we did in Ireland remains to be answered for.

At least they read me, you say. Yes, but at least is at

most. It goes in one ear and out the other, the ghost of a message moving from soul to soul.

Mine to theirs, if they had one. But they don't, or don't seem to. Only a set of senses, wanting a stimulus.

5

There are many circuits in an old house. In an old country, too, for that matter. Wires and pipes going everywhere. People who know people who know people who know people. It's a tangled skein.

We started early, the morning after the loss of the railings. You have to get your teeth in. The longer you leave it alone, the more you have to do. So we took a look at the electricity.

You know far more about it than I do. Those years making bombs for the government – or whatever you did – were a big help. You stood there in the freezing dungeons, running the theory over on your fingers, beautiful as a race-horse in your flying-jacket with its black fur lining.

Harland was beside us, a dour, stalwart silence. He was blue as a submarine in his boiler suit, the inevitable cigarette scoring a line of fire in the cold.

What had led us down here was a charred switch, and a strip of black scorching along a wall.

You could hardly believe the switch was made of wood. I put on the mock voice of a news-commentator when we discovered this atrocity, striking an attitude in front of an old wireless microphone.

'This was within spitting distance of the twenty-first century,' I said, sepulchral and sinister. 'And they were still using plinth switches carved from the primeval oaks of the Irish bog.'

That was a good day for me. Must have been. I was

flippant and cheerful, full of fun as an egg. But it didn't last.

'It'll have to be disconnected,' you said, ignoring me. 'I can't think how they took the risk. It's crazy.'

So we began work on the circuits, drawing deductions, tracing lines to boxes. It took us a while to find the right one, a set of open handles at the spring of an arch.

There were no windows in the corridor. Only bare stone flags and peeling whitewash, and the beam of a failing torch.

'Strike a light, Harland,' I called, hearing my voice dwindle, the echo of an order.

But Harland was close to my elbow, juggling a handful of miniature stone milk bottles.

'Fuses,' I suggested, not sure of my guess, but still proud enough to voice it aloud, an amateur with a sense of intuition.

How it was before, how it always will be. From the subaltern to the colonel, the lead of reason. But Aristotle and all his know-how still rests with the sergeant-major.

I took one of the fuses from Harland's hand, a cartridge of power.

'There are four or five sorts,' he was saying. 'The trouble is we have only this kind left, and I don't think it's the one you need.'

It wasn't, of course. But it took an hour of your fiddling and reasons, and two step ladders, to make sure.

I could see how much you hated Harland being right, and without having done the checks. Remorselessly, you went round the corridors, eliminating outside chances, testing possibilities you knew were unreal.

'I agree, Harland,' you said, at last.

We went over the distance to the hardware shops, how much petrol we had, the state of the weather, with a wind ripping branches off the trees. It was too far, it was too late.

So we took the same risk as the others, left the wooden switch in its vulnerable place.

'There are faults everywhere,' said Harland, over a pot of tea. 'You can always get a shock. The important thing is to keep your eyes open.'

That was when the telephone rang, another circuit. Harland went over to answer the call for me, a diligent footman. He picked up the receiver as if he expected it to explode. He may have been wise, or brave. One did explode once, in my cousin's office.

'It's Sean Lefroy,' said Harland.

'Returning your call,' said Sean, sharp as a bread-knife, when I took the basin, and pressed the buttons.

I checked the wavering hologram of his face in the eye-piece. Then I put the machine on secure.

You were offering Harland a slice of flan, the dilute green of passion-fruit and a skin of glue. But he eats like all the Irish, only meat and cheese, with a dash of cream. He shook his head.

'The railings have gone,' I said succinctly. 'I assume that you're on secure, as I am.' Then, hearing him say that he was, I went on. 'One arc was taken last night, with a laser saw. The other, I'm sure, will soon go.'

'Itinerants,' he suggested, the way I'd done myself.

But he listened carefully while I told him what Harland knew, the boasts of O'Neill, the potential guilt of the Desmond brothers.

'O'Neill's back in the north,' he said, after a while. 'Don't ask me how I know. But I'll make enquiries, John. I'll call you back. Leave it with me.'

Sean had a way of making everything seem easy. You left it with him, and he pulled a string or two, and what had seemed like a knot became an open door.

We drank our tea.

'How does he know O'Neill is back in the north?' I asked aloud, wondering.

34

Harland laughed.

'He had a drink with a garda who had a drink with another garda,' he said. 'The guards have been watching O'Neill for years. He has a conspicuous car, and he makes no secret of where he's going. Most of the time,' he added, swallowing the last of his tea.

'But the other bit of the time,' you said, watching Harland. 'That's the one that matters, isn't it?'

'Circuits within circuits,' I suggested, smiling. 'The Irish talk to the Irish, and the British talk to the guards.'

But I noticed that Harland didn't smile back.

Later that night we talked about him, while we undressed for bed.

'Another view of the milk mountain,' you joked, stripping your new bra, the one you wore now for the weight. 'The baby's kicking hell out of me.'

I went over and stood behind you, kissing your neck.

'The same as Harland is,' I said, softly.

But you pulled away, angry at the comparison.

Outside the window, the wind rose, rattling the glass in its pane. Swept through the arrowslit, and stirred the arras.

'Harland knows too much,' you said, throwing turf on the fire, turning towards me, light as a swallow still on your slim legs.

'We could die of suspicion,' I said, wanting to drop the subject, knowing that what I said was true. 'You have to trust someone, Liz. Beyond ourselves, I mean.'

But then there was no-one beyond ourselves, or between ourselves. Only our bodies moving, and the child in the womb, whom I felt move, and that was the first time I felt it move.

'My baby,' I said, and you let the ambiguity stand.

In the morning, we tried another circuit. I was feeling restless. It was a bright day, still windy and sometimes

35

wet, but not one to make you think of electricity. So we turned our minds to the pipes.

There had been a heating system, and a silver linkage of tubes through every room. Tall radiators, armoured with graduated screws, watched over corners, and hid themselves, just free of shutter-swing, under lofty windows.

The one that worried you had an oil-drum leaning against it, and a splash of orange grease over what might once have been a gaping wound, a scar in the flow.

They filled the house like a protecting army, it seemed. And here was one wounded, but still alive, and bleeding.

What had flowed through their veins had become corrupted, and gashed the surface, breaking through. Where there was one hole, there might soon be more. You can't be too careful. You have to assume the stress, the corrosion.

'Don't you, John?'

I agreed with you, standing in my bomber jacket, fingering the magnificent relief engraving on the surface of the metal, a rococo jungle of coiling lines.

'They're so beautifully made,' I said. 'If only we still had the time for this kind of craftsmanship.'

You were elsewhere, though, in the land of truth, not beauty.

'It'll have to be closed off,' you said, fiercely. 'The whole system. What's come out here may come out elsewhere, too.'

You were looking left and right, Cromwellian against the innocent radiators. This one had shown some weakness, and those might, too. There must be Draconian checks.

That was when Sean called.

'You're not going to like this, John,' he warned me. 'There's a new bungalow, a big one. Along the Galway Road. I recommend that you take a look at its gates.'

He might have said a barn, a palisade. A fort in the mountains.

'Tell me more,' I said, knowing the worst.

'They're black, of course. But they've just gone up, and they're old. And they're spears, the same pattern as yours. He's a cousin of Paul Desmond's, a building contractor.'

He might have been a bandit, a horse-thief. I felt all the guilt and grief in me disappear and well up into hatred and rage.

'The plundering swine,' I said. 'Can we sue him?'

But the voice of reason was droning on, with its qualifications, its ifs and buts, its iron mask on the mouth of vengeance.

'Now, John. I told you you wouldn't like this. He's a building contractor, a demolition expert. He has access to old railings, you can bet he has invoices and witnesses, too. There are plenty of railings shaped like spears.'

I stood looking out through the windows across the lake, towards the leafless trees, a pair of ponies grazing.

'They're trying to provoke you, John. They know you can't sue. Be careful.'

'Thanks, Sean,' I said. 'I'll be careful. But I'd like my revenge.'

Selfish, vindictive, they are; lawless and drunken. I picked up a small Japanese bowl, would have smashed it in anger.

Then I went through to the dining-room, saw your controlled fury against the heating system, still poised in anticipation, a British square.

I went downstairs, light heels on stone, opened the great engine-room doors and stood with Harland, in awe of the boiler. A rusting iron cube, on legs like a bath, it had once run on solid fuel, now ate up oil.

So I'd been told. It hadn't worked for years, not since Martin Dooley, the rock star, had been thrown across the

37

room, trying to light it. That was why he'd sold the house and the land, to the man who'd sold it to me.

Now there was a new boiler, that heated the water only, and this old monster, with its network of silver tubes all over the house, lay neglected and forgotten.

'There are engineers,' Harland agreed, when I asked about a servicing. 'You could get him going, easily enough. But you'd never afford to run the bugger. He'd cost you a thousand a month, more maybe.'

I looked at the suit of armour, sensed the sleeping warrior inside. I could understand why it seemed human to Harland, a creature with an appetite.

'So we'll close off the radiators,' I said, imagining a massacre of the loyal, a betrayal of faithful servants.

I thought of the brooks in Ireland, running with blood. We had fed them with swords. Now the guilt was coming back to its own, leaving them with a skin disease.

'Drain them,' I said suddenly, compassionate and hopeful. 'Perhaps we can find a way to narrow the circuit, reduce the costs.'

I had my vision of a small Praetorian guard, a few rooms running on the old heat, an oil-fired pale at the heart of the cold Republican house.

I went outside, struck the twin drums with the knob of my twisted shelalegh. Struck them again, again. Hearing the sound resound, like the beat from an orange lodge. As it would come, as it had already come and gone.

'Dry as a bone,' said Harland, phlegmatic. 'They've taken the lot. It's a wonder they've left the old drums on their legs. They'll be back for those, give them a chance.'

I listened to the echo of the shelalegh's music, the hollow clangour I had sent out across the forest like a kind of challenge. Flat of my hand on the metal, beat of my stick on the skin.

'You mean they come this close?' I asked, lowering my voice, not wanting you to hear.

'They did,' said Harland, seriously. 'They might not now.' Then, staring at the cats as they patrolled the yard. 'It might help if you got a dog. Something that would make a noise, if a man came near.'

So the idea of Hengist was born, the philosopher-king with a barrel round his neck.

I went indoors, and the days of the circuits were over. I found you clutching your stomach, a prisoner to indigestion.

'Not cross are you?' you asked, frowning up at me. 'The baby needed more coffee. More than I like, I mean.'

I shook my head, smiling.

'We're going to get a dog,' I said, watching the seven stars of Orion, the beheaded soldier falling south. 'It'll rock the baby to sleep.'

'Hengist, yes,' you said, creating his name, and that night I dreamed of Hengist, in full cry at the head of his pack of hounds, hunting the Desmonds and all their cousins to a grisly death.

Impaled at the last on their own gates, my railings.

6

We parked the car, and went in out of the sleet, uneasily. Not knowing who might be there, or why. But who was there surprised me.

The room was heavy with cigarette smoke, Riley's atmosphere. A television set in the corner, on perpetual blink. Some politician raging, Charlie, or Essex, it doesn't matter.

Then a small dapper man in a black coat was rising from beside the peat fire, his arm out in a courteous gesture.

'Madam,' he said.

You were quicker on the uptake than I had been, seconds ahead.

'Thank you, Mr O'Neill,' you said frigidly. But you took the stool he was offering, and stretched your hands to the blaze.

There were four or five of them around the fire, bandits and wayfarers, the way there had been for centuries. Declan, too, behind the bar, phlegmatic and wary. They all had short shots of whiskey, Paddy's or poteen, coupling them with pints of Guinness in the big stone vernacular flagons that were still popular.

'Long time, no see, John,' said O'Neill, staring at me with that shifty, speculative gaze of his. 'How's your cousin Tom?'

Tom had died in an ambush, three years ago by that night, and O'Neill knew this, but it didn't stop him turning the knife in the blood.

Now he was introducing people, not waiting for me to react. Martin Green, a Fitzgerald, Paul Desmond.

I nodded, watching you shiver towards the flames. We'd come down to the pub like Greeks trailing an olive branch. I wasn't here to make enemies, or start a fight, or quarrel. I saw this night as a kind of reconnaissance, a flight over no-man's land.

You don't expect the seven deadly sins, though, in your friendly local.

'What'll you both drink?' said O'Neill.

But I wasn't going to be bought by him.

'I've ordered,' I said rudely, signing to Declan. 'The usual, please.'

Declan had the Famous Grouse out on the counter, both tots. But O'Neill was reaching over, passing yours in his ringed, waxy fingers, before I could move. He didn't miss a trick.

'It's good to have you back,' O'Neill was saying. 'I hear you have a lovely house, John. That's wonderful for you both.'

I grunted, offended by his oily consideration.

'I was in the church up in Armagh,' O'Neill was continuing. 'The one your friend Philip wrote his poem about. Bejamus, there was a hero. Eh, Paul?'

There was a chorus of sycophantic approval around the fire, a pavane for a dead enemy.

'Indeed so,' said Paul Desmond, the first violin.

'He wrote the poem in England,' I said steadily. 'It's a joke about the Irish sixpence.'

I remember you looking at me, a warning look. There might be guns under their coats, or knives. They were loose and big enough.

O'Neill took a pull of his Guinness.

'Is that so, now?' he said, equably. 'No doubt you're right, sure. But I always thought he had Ulster in mind.'

The door of the pub opened, and a gust of sleet flared

in. Framed in the doorway was one of the new gardai, a machine pistol over his shoulder. But he didn't seem to see O'Neill, or care. He went over to the bar and ordered a Murphy's.

'What with so many dead lying around,' said O'Neill, finishing his analysis, draining his glass.

I meant to say that it wasn't a political poem, though I had my doubts. But instead I tried to shift the conversation, wanting him off my friends.

I stared at the green back of the guard, sipping whisky. You were doing the same on your stool, a safe prop for my calm.

'What are you doing now?' I asked. 'What brings you south, Hugh? Is it antiques, or trench mortars?'

'This and that, Spencer,' he said, smiling, making me wince.

I hate being wrong-footed over a social closeness.

'I travel to and fro. I'm a poor itinerant now, you know. A man in a caravan, one of the lords of the roads.'

There was a general laugh at this, but it didn't last long. The pub was filling up with a serious crowd, a darts team and their flashy women.

'I hear you're wanting to buy a dog, something to guard the house,' Paul Desmond said.

He was a fat, flabby man, with a tweed cap and wellingtons. I didn't like the look of him. He struck me as a gamekeeper trying to mimic a duke.

'Have you one to sell?' I asked.

'You never know.'

I took my life in my hands, hating the bastard.

'I hope it's not the sort that would cock its leg against someone else's railings.'

O'Neill had his hand on Desmond's arm, the knuckles showing white. A silence had fallen, the sort of silence that always falls in a pub when people know that a fight is about to start.

42

The guard had left, of course. They always have. But nothing happened, owing to Declan, maybe.

'Fitzgerald here,' he said, with a cough. 'John Fitzgerald was saying we ought to call a meeting, about the gravel for the road.'

It defused the tension. Swords were being replaced in scabbards, the sawdust was no longer breathing blood. So Declan laughed.

'The sort of job for Riley.' he said. 'The great organizer. I remember the day he had us all planting beech-trees for barrel-staves.'

O'Neill was lighting a Gaulloise, inhaling the smoke like a French gangster in a film. He always seemed to see himself as if the cameras were turning, a knack he had picked up from Riley in Dublin, when Riley was still the model they all followed.

'I hear the man's doing time in London,' he said, with a grin. 'O'Rahilly in chains. It's hard to imagine.'

'His name's Riley,' you said quietly, forestalling me. 'You know that very well, Neil.'

Somewhere out of the corner of my eye I could see a boy slipping a ball from the pool table into the toe of a stocking. Glass would be breaking soon. Jagged edges going for eyes.

But O'Neill was calm, spreading his hands.

'It's one country now, Lady Spencer,' he said. 'We may have to swap names, like everything else. Gulp a bit of the wrong pronunciation down with our Guinness. Yesterday's men are in prison, you see.'

But Riley was never one of yesterday's men. You thought of Riley, you thought of something not yet invented, even then. He was always evasive, energetic, riding the whirlwind with a knife in his teeth, a new metre under his glove.

I remembered him once entering this very pub when O'Neill was only a name in an H-block.

43

'Drinks all round,' he said, like Wayne in a western, laying doubloons on the wood.

Every man I could see had swallowed Riley's hospitality, then his orders. He could make a nation eat from his hand.

'Let's go, Liz,' I said, emptying my glass.

Declan beckoned me, though, and I walked along the bar, leaning towards him. His curling hair was like flies in molasses.

'Peter Clancy here will take a share,' he said, nudging a bony man at his elbow. 'So will some others. After all, it's a common road. No reason you should pay for the gravel all yourself.'

'We can pay,' you said, fiercely. 'That is, if we have to.'

'I'm sorry,' Declan murmured, lowering his eyes. 'O'Neill won't always be here, you know. He's passing through.'

I took a last look round the little pub, the smoky rafters, the flyblown posters announcing rat poison, forgotten hurling matches.

Then we were out in the sleet and the wind, looking left and right, feeling the great absences under the thatch, hearing the doped adolescents revving their super tens on the bypass.

It took the car a while to start, a security risk. When the engine caught, I saw Paul Desmond smiling and beckoning. I ran the window down.

'Congratulations to you both,' he said. 'Let's hope it's a boy.'

Then he turned away, laughing.

7

We were up in Lancashire, I remember. That's when it came to a head, and there was nothing left for us, nothing but come home to Ireland.

You flee your *doppelgänger*, she's there behind you, in all the mirrors. In front of you, too. But I had to try, or lose what matters.

I'd been reading poems on a course, seeing Riley about a meeting in Westminster. I don't remember. Anyway, there'd been work, and now there was play. We were in a cold stone farmhouse on the moors, adapted for students.

Rebellion had come and gone. Now there were big windows, beds with duvets. The usual habitat plainness.

If I see another stripped pine wardrobe, I'll go crazy, for real. That's what I think sometimes, after those courses. Hair shirts on the mind, straw mats on the floors.

'I could take their bloody puritanism and shake its legs off. Organic form and all.

'Tell you, now. But for the penalties, hell fire and what not, I could go for the bell, book and candle brigade. The Pope in Rome and his marble minions.'

That's what Riley said, the day he came out, after seven muesli breakfasts and a week of blue stockings and home-weave stories.

You knew the score, but you came. Elephant's grass in the yard, laurustinus on the drive. It must have been February.

So we sat over mugs of Bailey's. We'd been making the

45

double bed, and then it struck you. Struck us both, perhaps.

'She was here, wasn't she? Here, I mean. Here in this room.'

Yes, was the answer. Yes, of course she was. You know that she was, and you did know.

But I didn't want to be quite so clear. I was frightened.

Then you compressed your lips, and threw the duvet on the floor, and kicked the mattress.

'Here in this filthy little sub-walnut surrogate for a fuck-space.'

'Very good,' I suggested, striving to joke my way through.

But it was the wrong move.

You went over to the replacement fire, working the copper hood to and fro, in a rage.

There was rain falling, glass rods of it. Wind on the hills. A Lancashire winter. Easy to remember the same rain, seven years ago, and the bloody mouse of my child.

Linda thin as a rake, after the operation. Stooping and vulnerable. The pain of congress, the closeness of shared evil.

I tried to put my arm on your shoulder, wiping away the treacherous cobwebs. But you froze, and then shrank inwards, a furious, defended snail.

'Forgive me,' I tried. 'I love you so very much. But I can't eliminate the past. It's like tattered veils in your mind. You see whatever I do through a gauze of torment.'

It was half an hour, though, before you would speak. When you did speak, the words were like iron out of your mouth.

'I can't go on,' you said.

Swallowing cream and whiskey, swilling it round. Tight-lipped, sure of your mind.

'She's everywhere,' you said. 'Everywhere we go, it's

46

as if she's painted the walls in her blood. You can't forget her. She's there with you.'

'Nonsense,' I said, uneasily. 'It's not me, it's you.'

But it wasn't. Linda was still there like a burning sore in those days. Later, too, we know she was. But I didn't dare to admit this.

I needed something to fiddle with. I had a little leather case for my hair-brushes, and I started to press the brass clasp of it in and out with my forefinger and thumb.

'Keep still,' you said softly. 'It's all right.'

You were like that. Always, even then. You could move from a fierce mood to a gentle one, like an eye rolling.

I must have been very tense. You could tell something had to give. So you put your hand on my hand, full of love. But you didn't loose your grip.

Outside the rain changed into sleet, sheeting down like metal. Inside, there was ice in the air, still.

'It's like this,' you said, very calm. 'I do mind, and I may exaggerate. I agree. But I haven't known you long. So listen. You and I are like twin funnels on a great ship, the Titanic, say. But Linda's like an iceberg, and she's mostly underwater. I can't see her, and she could sink us. What she was, what she is.'

It was true, it was clever. I listened, admiring you, knowing already how well you understood me, how much you were going to mean.

'Think of those poems,' you said. 'All sheep-shit and shepherds. Pastorals, yes. But the real message is you with your hands on the cow's udders of imagination, milking out your love for Linda. Linda, Linda, Linda, like a little clinking bell. No wonder it worries me.'

Then you took a long draught of the mud in your glass, and it came out, the main worry.

'You say you love me. But where are my poems?'

It takes time. The raw material goes into the mincer, it comes out like a string of sonnets. Here they are, bound

47

in fine calf, your name on the title page, signed by my quill.

But they weren't written, that afternoon in Lancashire. It was hard. I took you into my arms, kissing your neck, scratching the small of your spine under your blouse, the way you like.

'They'll come,' I promised. 'Never fear.'

But you put me aside, walking over to the streaming pane, staring out across the valley, across a future littered with obstacles and challenges.

Then you turned, a sudden spindle of decision.

'It isn't the poems,' you said. 'Not really. They're just a symptom. The problem is here. Lancashire, England. Everywhere you've been with Linda. It's got a stain over it, I can't live with it.'

The room was cold now, bone-dry, the heating off, the light not on. I got up and switched a bedside lamp's button, flooded a small glowing cone onto the floor.

'We must get away,' you said. 'Somewhere fresh.'

The room seemed to gather into a pile of sticks, waiting for a match to kindle a blaze. I cleared my throat, prompting you.

'Scotland, maybe?'

'Scotland's too dangerous. Too expensive. Besides you were there with Linda.'

'Where, then? I was everywhere with Linda. You know I was.'

'You were never in Ireland.'

The fencing was over, I had my back to the wall, the glass of Bailey's draining in my fist. There was nowhere else, I knew. Linda and I had cleared the east, there was only the west, its tensions, its memories.

But you were spelling it out.

'It has to be Ireland. I was born there, we met there, we were happy there. It has to be Ireland.'

I couldn't begin to tell you, not then, how Linda was

only part of the trouble, how Ireland was full of so many other ghosts.

'I could speak to Riley,' I said. 'Or Philip. They might be able to put in a word with the syndicate in Munster. We could get a loan, perhaps. Buy a small estate with a castle.'

Then you had turned a small cartwheel, acrobatic in that high room, were kneeling at my feet, serious.

'You're all right, aren't you?'

'I'm all right,' I assured you. 'I'm really fine.'

'I'm sorry I was manky.'

Precious jewels were pouring out of a box, legions of tenderness fondling the rough places in my nerves.

'I'll speak to my father,' you said. 'He might be able to help with some china, some contacts.'

'I'll speak to Riley,' I said.

So that Ireland was born already, growing into an ashlar house. A fort by a lake. Kneeling to atone.

8

Up on the roof, you could see a long way. I had my binoculars out, an army pair, 1944, with camouflage iron sides and a cross hair in the lenses. I could say they were a desert pair. But they weren't, alas.

I doubt if they ever trained on anything more dangerous than a land-girl in a field near Aldershot. Not until they came over to Ireland, anyway. But I had them now on the Hill of Slaughter, that miasma of blood.

I shifted the focus, bringing the far farms in, the pylons. Watching the near sheep and their dark lambs. It was raining hard, and I had to keep the hood of my anorak up.

Harland and I were on the slates below the front ridge. A long gulley, floored with lead, ran along the middle of the roof, and the slopes on either side gave this area the effect of an infantry trench.

It reminded me of what Riley would always answer, if you asked him casually what he was doing.

'Keeping my head below the parapet. Appreciating the situation.'

He had a taste for military metaphors, even in boyhood. When his father came home from the war with a cache of Nazi insignia, he became a connoisseur of the SS. The defeated always appealed to Riley, like the sense of siege.

I noticed that Harland was saying something, breaking into my thoughts.

'I'm sorry,' I said. 'I didn't hear.'

The wind rose, battering into my face, justifying this

failure. But it cut no ice with Harland. He repeated what he had said, mouthing aloud and clear towards my ear.

He always treated me as if I was going deaf, particularly out of doors, or when there was background noise.

Perhaps I was going deaf. So much had happened already in those days. But you never quite confirmed his diagnosis.

'You didn't listen,' you said. 'That's the trouble.'

'A dog,' Harland was saying. 'I think I can get you a dog.'

Nobody was in sight. Only the trees moving, the wildfowl coming in to rest on the lake. Furrowing the water with the draught of their wings.

Ridiculously, I half expected to see a tangled mongrel trotting up the drive, keeping its head down against the wind. Something that Harland had conjured out of the air and the bracken, a wizard of provision.

But this was just one of his shifts of tack, a typical device. We had come up on the roof in pursuit of the third circuit, a means to clear the chimneys. Here in the gulley, while I took a look round with my glasses, Harland had let his mind move to a new theme.

I gestured to him, and we walked along to the end of the gulley where the slope of three roofs formed a small space with more shelter.

'I was talking to one of the itinerants,' Harland said, wiping rain from his eyes. 'They have a puppy to sell, a big dog. I forget the breed.'

Above us the main chimney stack towered, the periscope on a nuclear submarine. A battleship in enemy waters, that's what we were. A cleaving, grey menace.

Then I remembered. It was only rain. They were only fields. The people were friendly, give them a chance. This wasn't the bloody world of the eighties. Tom King, Tom Gray.

51

You come back to learn, to fraternize, you have to try. But it wasn't easy.

'It has to be stolen,' I said, forcing my thoughts back to Harland and his dog. 'I mean, they always are, aren't they? Things they sell.'

Harland was nodding, water glazing the gold of his oiled sou'wester, a dripping monk on sentry duty. I smiled, seeing myself the same way. No lifeboat rescues today.

The weather gets so bad, you just have to grit your teeth and grin. It stops everything.

'Let's go down,' I said. 'We'll come back up when it's dry.'

So we lurched into the gusts, through the clacking door and onto the rafters, where it was calmer. Only the trickle of runnels and the scuff of crows.

I went first through the trap-door and down the aluminium ladder, waiting for Harland in a pool of water on the upper landing.

'It's a good dog,' said Harland, leaning on the balustrade at the top of the stairs, 'A nice bark. He would do the job well for you.'

'But stolen.'

'You see,' said Harland, ignoring this, 'they have no use for the dog. He'll be going cheap.'

Harland looked up at the lotus, where a chandelier had once hung, where a ring of blazing torches had swung over nightlong carousing.

'They won't want to feed him much longer,' he said, shaking his head. 'If they don't get a sale, they'll kill the beast.'

I took my coat off, laying it over the banister, looking down.

'I can't take a stolen dog,' I said, knowing I could. 'Who was the owner? Where is it from?'

Harland was inspecting his nails.

'The other side of Ireland,' he suggested. 'Anywhere. Who knows? I mean,' he added, helping me forward. 'It might not be stolen. It might have been thrown out, abandoned. It happens every Christmas.'

'Get them to bring it round,' I said. 'I'll have a look at the dog. Mind you, I'm not promising anything. Tell them that.'

'You'll not regret the dog,' said Harland, stepping over the remaining obstacles.

Then I began to wonder. Had Harland a commission from the tinkers? Was he in business with them? What else might I have to buy?

But it didn't matter. I couldn't know. So we went back to the chimneys, trying them one by one to see which flues would clear.

I thought how typical it was. Dogs and chimneys, bodyguards and railings. Always one problem interleaving with another, a kind of Irish sandwich.

The bodyguard had appeared again while I was on the phone to Sean, the day after our trip to the pub, when the snow started. Started and stopped, soon enough. But there was a thick flurry when you called me to the front door.

He was a small, wiry man, cracking his knuckles in a rusty Fiesta. He didn't get out, and I didn't ask him to. He had a soft, rasping voice.

'Thought you might need some protection,' he said.

Liverpool accent, look of a boxer.

'I'm not a rock star,' I said. 'I'm a writer, a retired civil servant.'

'I know,' he said. 'With the army.'

I didn't like that. I thought of Martin Dooley, his helicopter circling to land through the snow. Men with guns lining a path to show him to the door.

Flakes were landing on my hand, melting.

53

'Look,' I said. 'I'll be in touch. If I need someone, I'll let you know.'

He was scribbling something on the back of a card, his name, Jarlath Fahy, and then a series of numbers.

I flipped the card over. Address of a club, he must be a bouncer.

'Any time,' he was whispering, a greaseproof paper noise. 'Give me a call.'

Then he was gone, a monster retreating into a crystal ball. The snow went on for a while, and then it was gone, too. All that was left was a memory and a shadow, a hint of violence.

A dog would be cheaper, I thought. Less trouble, too, than a bodyguard. Then I left Harland screwing his forty rods together in the dining-room, hearing the phone ring.

It was Riley. It can't have been, but it was. I knew it was him before he spoke. You always did, with Riley.

'I'm out on bail,' he said. 'I'm coming over.'

'But surely,' I said. 'You can't leave the country, can you?'

Riley laughed.

'After the trial, of course.'

But in the event there was no trial. Riley came over a free man. There were settlements out of court, squarings of juries. Riley had his contacts, like O'Neill.

I suppose. I can't remember what else was said. It was one of so many times I thought he rang, saw his name on the back of a letter. I missed him so much.

But he never came. I mean, he did come, but I wasn't there. I don't know what I mean.

I took a pill, and went back to the chimneys, remembering the green chairs by the phone, the feel of the Black Prince in my lap.

'Wrong number,' I said.

I must have done. Riley or no Riley, I'd have said the same. I trusted Harland, but not with Riley's life.

It was one of those long Februaries. The snowdrops were everywhere, the daffodils not yet through. This was our third morning on the chimneys, and every morning we'd been driven back from the roof, unable to cope with wind or hail.

Two men had come with vacuum equipment, and one had cleared the hall. The other had said we'd have to dismantle the stacks, brick by brick. He'd asked for twenty pounds to pay for his petrol. But he cleared nothing.

So Harland and I had begun with the rods, flexible sticks with a screw on the end. They went up and up, or down and down, but then it was always the same. They came to an absolute block.

'It's the crows,' Harland said. 'We'll never beat them.'

At length we got one clear, a flue in a little room upstairs. A tiny fire of turf blazed in the grate, and Harland and I stood warming our hands.

A tea chest was full of twigs. Twigs and mud.

'The nests can be six feet deep,' said Harland. 'I can only pick them to bits piece-meal.'

But it was worse than that. Sometimes the flues bent, and the nests were built round the bend, and the rods were too short to reach, or too weak to break their hold.

We began on the soot-boxes, metal doors high up on the walls, put in to grant access to the bends. But they never seemed to be close enough, or they were concreted up, and we didn't always know which flue we were doing, or even if there was a fire at the end of the flue at all. Sometimes the rods rattled to a halt in walls where there was no grate.

These were the circuits of dirt, the conduits of a black secret enemy we could see every evening at twilight, scattered like burnt leaves in a raucous traffic above the trees.

'There's a curse on the house,' Harland said, on the fourth day. 'The landlord once refused a wise woman food in his kitchen. She said the day would come when the crows flew in and out of his doors.'

She was right, sure enough. But the crows flew in and out by their own passages, and we hadn't the means to clear them. I could hear their feet on the roof, like fingers scratching my skull.

'I don't believe in curses, Harland,' you told him, and you made us keep on trying.

We did clear a few fires, but it was bitter work. The end of the month brought an uneasy truce. We had some heat, and the crows still held their main roosts, and their access.

Tom Gray came into Ireland at the start of the bloody eighties, a force for change. The word is, he evaded the posting ten years earlier. He never wanted the job.

The end of the day, though, you take what you're given in the Diplomatic Service. You move, or you're out.

So Tom Gray, the Baron as he later was, assumed his baton and his demesne. He set up his headquarters in a ramshackle Victorian house on the outskirts of Belfast, a tower with batteries, and I had a suite of rooms in an outbuilding. That was the office, a former stables.

Gray had been wounded, and he came out of the Fusiliers with a limp and a temper. He carried a masking smile, and a bark like a Dobermann. They knew his kind, in London. Polite, but vicious.

Exactly what they need in the boondocks, they must have been saying in Whitehall. Must have been saying for years, for a century. So Tom Gray packed his trunks, and looked around for a staff.

He found what he wanted at the Army and Navy Stores, a gaggle of discontented, ambitious officers, and a raft of folding furniture. Campaigner's things. He didn't mean to be sitting still very much.

I knew Tom from my Cambridge days, when I used to go down to London and eat a meal in their little flat off Kensington High Street. He and his dry, military wife. They were starting young, going far.

The bright lights had started to shine in Africa. Now they were beckoning out of the bogs, and the Wicklow

Mountains. You dig deep enough in the peat, and find your medals. That was the thinking in those days.

I suppose it must have been mine, anyway. I can't imagine me signing on for five years in the west without some incentive, imaginary or otherwise. I needed exile from the Court and the Gate like a hole in my gall bladder.

I'd lost my chance in France, of course. I don't know why. It wasn't Philip's fault, a royal whim, perhaps, but Lester had let me down. The switchback eighties, that's the way they were. You're off today, home tomorrow.

So I sat one night in my room, fiddling limericks, adjusting Ariosto, and the phone rang. It was Tom, a dispenser of patronage.

Come to Ireland with me, John, that was the essence. I need a secretary. Then, when I must have been hesitating: 'You'll have your pickings, of course. Like all the rest of us.'

But no. He won't have said that. They never did. He'll have mentioned the Queen's need, the responsibility of the post, the fact I was indispensible. I was the only man he knew who could write.

So I said yes. I don't know why. His honeyed tongue, my being at a loose end. It doesn't matter. In two weeks I had my bags on the boat, and the ferry was ducking into a force ten gale.

The usual crossing. I won't go over it twice. But once I was through the nausea, it began to seem like a good idea. Land of opportunity, the emerald isle.

I had space for the first time, money, too. You could spend what you liked, the budget went on for ever. Hiring filing cabinets, engaging clerks. You signed the chit, Aladdin rubbing his lamp, and your will was done.

Later, things changed. But that was later. The days of the accountants had yet to dawn. Euphoria ruled for the first months, and I was basking under its light.

I could requisition a cottage, transfer a girl. We laid on

Fax, I had the office repapered. Walnut desks were installed, wall lighting.

It must have been then I met O'Neill. Running errands for Tom, or one of his confidantes. A local boy anxious to rise. Neat moustache like the Boss, and a coat cut in the latest London style.

I won't have noticed, though. I was too far up the ladder. Minding my own business, whatever that was, enjoying the power and the freedom. O'Neill was a clerk then, a nobody.

Life in the Pale was easy, a social round. You went to a party, you never saw an Irish face. The same young officers as in London went round in the same dances. The same girls giggled and kissed them. The same, or their doubles.

I could get what I wanted, and I enjoyed the life. Nobody crossed me, knowing Tom was my cousin. Plenty came twisting their caps in their hands, desiring favours. I liked saying yes, and sometimes I liked saying no, too. Cruelties follow their own occasions.

Of course, they blew up the Nelson Monument one bitter dawn, but I wasn't there. They threw a bomb into the military attaché's kitchen, but no-one was killed. You could hear about these things, read about them, but it made no difference. You were in a fortress, and it wasn't under siege.

Then one morning the September after we landed, three weeks in, I suppose, Tom held a meeting. Generals round a mahogany table, brandy or cream coffee, whatever you wanted. I took the minutes, the way I always did.

'They're a mile beyond Kinross,' Tom said, smoothing his paperknife in his fingers, a mannerism he had. 'Holed up in the woods. No more than two thousand, I hear. That right, Simon?'

Someone nodded, I forget who.

'There's a tree across the road. Flooding everywhere. It's time for a show of force.'

'They can cope with the floods,' a voice said, I'd better not say whose. 'Better than we can, Tom.'

But he wasn't listening. Tom Gray was in his Napoleon dream, scourging the rebels with one quick, incisive thrust, and returning home in triumph. To Belfast for a bath, and some television.

'We're saddled up,' he said, frowning towards the objector, prodding a blotter with his knife. 'I've given the orders.'

That was how it often was, later. An advisory committee turning into a press conference. Officers being invited to rubberstamp his decisions. But this was the first time.

A big marble clock with a Gorgon's head on the front in gold was ticking away on the mantelpiece. You could see the hawk eyes of someone's ancestors, but not Tom's, if you looked at the pictures.

Nobody looked anywhere. There was a long silence.

'Thank you, gentlemen,' Tom said, very quietly.

The following morning, two of the officers round the table were dead, assassinated in an ambush. The open Daimler Tom had ridden in was on its side in a ditch, and I was taking dictation on a shooting-stick.

Imagine sporadic firing. Very muddy khaki. The rifles jamming, a field telephone on the blink.

It wasn't my baptism of fire. There were shots exchanged in the north when I was a tutor. But I learned a lesson from this.

Never trust the General.

Tom was a shrewd man for despatches, though. I'll grant him that. He knew the way to make sure the paper work was accurate.

So there I see him, brushing blood – someone else's –

off his jodhpurs, rattling perfect sentences into the wind and the rain, for me to make a story out of.

That was why I was so important. I see it now, I began to see it then. I could weave a victory out of a failure, protect a narrative of defeat with extenuating circumstances.

Heroism, I see now, is the art of choosing tomorrow's poet. The dusty chronicles of squalid campaigns can be made to blaze into fine preferments. I know. I had plenty of practice.

'Outnumbered by better-armed forces,' Tom was saying, treating a swagger-stick like barley-sugar, a man sucking for inspiration. 'Seriously outnumbered, you'd better say. Our men gave an excellent account of themselves despite severe casualties.'

There was more of the same. Orderlies carrying men back from the front, with their guts hanging out. A cart of bodies, a sky of dud shells. The retreat in full swing.

I rode beside him all the way. Someone had set his arm in a sling, I don't know why, and he looked pretty good. Wearily courageous. A dogged fighter, ready for the next bout.

'There'll be another time,' he even called to an old woman waving, well inside the city perimeter.

I admire his gall, even now. Meanwhile that afternoon, my fiction was already on the wire to London, where those who needed to know, a powerful few, would soon be reading Tom Gray's version of what happened on the Border of Donegal.

A disaster, modulated as a skirmish. A catastrophe, from which a limited gain would be extracted. Not too extreme. After all, they would hear some other versions.

Just enough to suggest the ring of truth, the honesty of a calm analysis. I was good at this, and Tom Gray knew I was.

61

We had dinner together in The Silver Swan, a rack of lamb, and some oranges in cointreau.

'You did well, John,' Tom told me. 'You go to the heart of a situation. You're not fooled by surface appearances. You'll go far.'

Some quails in aspic. A mousse of sardines. Furnish your own meal. A belly dancer, maybe, a cloud of incense. Tom was being the genie of the lamp for me, the magician who opens all the doors.

'Have some Hollands,' he said, flooding the stuff in a beaker. 'You know, John, I've been thinking. You need your own house, more time for your writing. I can't have you going home because I'm keeping you too busy.'

Fat chance on a seven-year contract, I was thinking. Pay at the end, the bonus goes if you don't last.

'Have a word with a few estate agents. Ask for brochures.'

He smiled at me, he knew I felt flattered.

'Now that we're settled in, we can both take a long weekend occasionally. I could do with a break myself, and I'm sure you could use a Friday or two for your own work. We're all waiting for something special, you know. A Soldier's Calendar, shall we say?'

He laughed at his own joke, and I laughed with him. I mean, you had to with Tom. What else was there to do?

So I rented my bungalow, and I took my Fridays, the rewards of treason. I didn't like the price, but I liked the time and the space. I began to think, and then I began to plan.

I took them out an hour ago, from the box under the bed. Both volumes, the calf edition. The twisted fruits of a savage land.

There might have been more, there won't now. Tom Gray in his grave, though, and his false despatches, you could say without him there wouldn't have been what there is.

I began writing after the Eustace affair, putting it all in, the truth and the lies, an allegory for the times.

Twelve books, twelve cantos. A gross of rhymes bought with a mess of guilt.

10

W e took the outbuildings one at a time, the annexe, the mortuary chapel. But I have to stop there. The mortuary chapel was too much for me.

After a cup of coffee, and a breath of air in the yard, I felt I could go back in again.

It's a long building, was a barn once, I suppose. In the days of the old people, they laid the dead out there. There's a wooden block shaped like a coffin, lights all round, a smell that's hard to define.

Stale candlegrease, wet coats, airlessness. A smell of cheap scent and the unwashed bodies of priests.

And something else. The lost legion, the old who die and were mourned, Roncalli's regiment.

That's what brought it on, the Italian name coming to me, remembering Riley's telephone call. Roncalli's men, Ricaldi's, where's the difference?

'Sixty we had one year,' Harland told me, when I asked him. 'February was the worst, the wind and the cold. We had over a hundred cars once, for a wake.'

Sixty or six hundred, the numbers flicker. The slow cars moving away to the cemetery, the carts to the boneyard, the pits of lime.

I took you in with me, and we held hands, going through the rooms, and it was better. The room for the vestments, the little room with the air filter, the room for storing the chairs.

Then the smell, and the arches. The mortuary chapel

itself. A plaster angel on a window-sill, some art deco glass.

Riley would have gone right up to it, lain down with his hands crossed on his chest. He'd have made a joke of it, I know my Riley.

'The block'll have to go,' I said. 'Harland will have to move the block.'

You made me sit on a hard chair against the wall, facing the windows. A lawn-mower lay in a corner, the ruins of a pillow.

'The baby's irritating my skin today,' you said, sitting down beside me, normal and worried. 'Scratch my back, will you?'

So I put my hand up under your shirt on the bare lovely flesh, rubbing my fingers to and fro, like a comforting small animal.

'Don't worry about the block,' you said softly. 'Don't worry about anything.'

The flakes of skin from your back came away in my hands, and the chapel became a barn again. But not the barn it had been, the other barn, where the straw would never be cleansed of blood.

'It's got to be done,' Tom Gray was saying, slapping his breeches with his driving gloves.

It was three months after the ambuscade in the gully, a panicky November. Inside the City, all was calm, a winter season of comfits and dancing. But elsewhere, everything was shaken about.

Tom had it all in hand. A dose of his inspiration and my neat handwriting, and all was well. A quiet London, a happy Minister.

But not even Tom and his flair for propaganda could write off a cell of foreign guerrillas in a British port.

So we drove a hundred miles, from Belfast to the coast. Stopped to shoot some peasants. There was always shooting.

65

'Got to make an example,' said Tom, before a shoot. 'Show the flag, you know.'

So we did some execution. Took a few peasants here and there, bandits. Put their backs against walls. But there were formalities, forms to be filled in. It was quite regular, according to the book.

Those that we punished were criminals, and they had their trials. Wigs were worn, defence and then prosecution. A colour of justice.

We reached the port on the heels of our reputation, a disciplined force. The guerrilla unit was in a safe house on the edge of the town, a fortress with loopholes.

We put a boom across the bay, cut them off. But they were disillusioned already, disappointed by what was waiting. No Dr Sanders with a thousand men. No money and supplies.

Tom requisitioned a farmhouse where we ate a fair supper, beef and mustard. He had a cigar going, and was warming his hands at a log fire when they brought an Ambassador in. Under a white flag, of course. But he took a risk.

'You speak English?'

'Some.'

'What are you? Red Brigade, or a free lance?'

'Neither.'

'Now see here.' And this is where you had to admire Tom Gray. He knew how to handle this kind of interrogation. He had his own way from the start, throwing some more wood on the fire, tapping ash out, as if he had all the time in the world.

I just sat there taking notes, the witch's familiar. A man in black, with a book.

'We know exactly who you are. How many of you there are, and why you're here. Now tell me. You've been let down, haven't you?'

The Ambassador nods. I see him nodding now, a slim dark face like a raven's, eager to please.

'Course you have. Happens to all of us, one time or another. Bloody shame'

Flames flickering on the rafters, Tom rubbing his riding boots, the voice of the confessional.

'Is all a mistake. We give you no trouble.'

'No,' said Tom, smiling to himself. 'I'm sure you won't. You've lost your money, and that's that. As for your little Italian friends, who fancy it's mafia time here in Ireland, you just go back and tell them it's no dice. No dice and no incense, either. You pass your arms over, and you come out with your hands in the air, and we may just forget the visa problems.'

'You mean, we surrender, you put us on a plane?'

'I can't promise anything.'

But he made it sound as if he could. Oh yes, he made it sound as if he could promise the moon, he had the power.

'I tell them. And, thank you, sir.'

So the following morning, a fair day, a surprise for November, we stood in the barn, the sun coming in.

Several of us, I don't know how many. The witnesses. Tom was in a belted raincoat. It seemed to accentuate his limp, making him archetypal, a provincial rep lead having a go at Richard the Third.

O'Neill, was he there? I sometimes wonder. He can't have been, though, he wasn't senior enough. But he'd have heard the story, it went round the office.

'Nearly time,' Tom was saying, glancing at his watch. 'They ought to be here.'

Then there was the sound of a car, and I saw a black limousine drawing up in the yard. The double doors of the barn were open, and I had a good view of it, the panels glossy, the hubs flecked with mud. But there was no mistaking what it was.

Two young soldiers got out of the front, wary, moving

their guns. Then the back slid open, and an officer dropped out from behind the coffin.

Caught his balance, and saluted. Immaculate as on parade, with a pistol in a holster. A sub-machine gun, a sword, what's the difference?

It was Riley, right enough. Addressing Tom Gray as General, I could hear, waving his arm towards the safe house.

'Lieutenant Riley,' Tom had told me earlier. 'He'll be arranging the details. You'll meet him later. A good man, and he writes a bit of poetry, too.'

None of us went forward to speak to Riley. We didn't want to, at this stage. You hire an executioner, you let him get on with his work.

Someone handed round a flask, a full colonel with his hands trembling. Then Tom Gray came back inside, and watched the car drive away, and made the remark I remembered.

'It's got to be done.'

Later we heard the shots, a half dozen, and then a *coup de grâce*. You kill six or six hundred, it's much the same. Swords flashing, men scream, blood on the cuffs.

None of us said anything when we heard the shots. None of us said much at all. Tom had a camp stool in a corner, was reading something, Tacitus, or Baedeker. The rest of us just stood in the straw, waiting.

Then there was the noise of a car's engine, and I heard it stop in the yard. The doors were still open, and they brought the first coffin in, four of them, gasping under the weight, Riley guiding the thing on its eight legs, like a siege engine, towards a trestle.

There were five others, lining the far wall, the coffins beside them on the floor.

'Lieutenant Riley,' Tom was saying, hoisting himself up from the camp stool. 'I'd like you to meet my secretary, my cousin, John Spencer.'

So we were introduced, and we shook hands over the body of a mercenary, whom Riley had just despatched with his Colt revolver, like a hog on a hook.

'Spencer,' he said, staring at me out of his grey eyes. 'You must be the poet. I'd like to see more of you, after this.'

He had real admiration in his voice. That's the main thing I remember. That and the fleck of red on his sleeve.

Then they were loading the next coffin, an empty one, into the hearse, and the process was going on, as it had to, five hundred more times.

Five times, or fifty. It doesn't matter. The mortuary carts grinding over the cobbles towards the mass grave.

They surrendered their weapons, and with them they surrendered their lives. Their bodies were ours to dispose of, according to the custom of the age.

It was Tom, of course, who delivered the funeral speech, when the last coffin was in place on its trestle.

'These people were terrorists,' he said. 'They came from a foreign country, either for pay, or out of fanaticism. Their job was to maim or kill, to subvert the peaceful lives of ordinary men and women.'

Tom paused for a moment there, laying his hand on the brass handle of one of the coffins.

'They got what they deserved,' he said, quietly. 'Their bodies will be cremated, and their ashes scattered. That ends the matter. The remaining details will be attended to by Lieutenant Riley and his men.'

Tom looked at his watch, then took a turn up and down the barn. He had our attention.

'Gentlemen,' he said. 'It is now three forty-five, precisely. You will each now, and this is an order, erase from your minds whatever has happened during the last one hour and a half. Is that understood?'

We all nodded, I suppose. He was charismatic, all right.

'There will be a report, of course. It should be in your

69

hands in one hour's time. I shall expect you all to have memorized its wording, and I mean its wording, not its substance, before we meet for dinner. John, shall we go indoors?'

In the farm kitchen, he stood in front of the stove, lifting his coat tails and warming his buttocks. Then he dictated the famous letter, more or less as I have it here.

'Accompanied by a small expeditionary force, I invested the port and made a house to house search; but could find no evidence of any foreign intervention, neither men, weapons nor supplies. In my opinion the rumour of a landing by a mercenary contingent is entirely imaginary.'

'You see, John,' he said, lighting himself the first cigar of the evening, 'there are bleeding hearts everywhere, even in Whitehall. You can't be too careful. They want their stables cleaned, but they don't want to read a sorry tale of how dirty they were.'

So that was what happened. Nothing, it seems. It wasn't the only time I remembered the nothing, sitting holding your hand and scratching your back in the mortuary chapel, but it was the first.

The first, or the worst. One of them, anyway. It came back in dreams, too, and I used to wake and scream. Then it came back when I met Riley again, in Belfast and elsewhere. It always does.

I see Riley as the executioner. He can execute anything, a commission, an order, a human being. It doesn't matter. He does it with skill, and tact. You turn away, and you hate him, and then he smiles, and you love him again, bringing you houses, power, money.

Tom Gray, the voice, and Riley, the iron hand. They made a pretty pair.

11

Hengist came one afternoon in a superannuated Ford, a Granada, I think. Some kind of rustbucket with a super-charger that made a noise like a de Lorean.

Or perhaps it just had a broken exhaust. It had been a busy day, and I wasn't really ready. The prospective maid, whom I'd forgotten, had been delivered after lunch by her husband, and we were just recovering.

A bony long-jawed woman, with staring eyes and an itch, she'd nibbled a roll and a few Abernethy biscuits, refusing tea.

Her eyes had gone through mine and out the other side. But they didn't seem to see anything. She stared like a blind woman.

'One day a week,' you were saying. 'Perhaps two.'

I could see you were thrown by this lean witch, as I was. But she came with Harland's blessing, and a reputation for hard work and honesty.

'You have to pick and choose them,' Harland had warned us. 'You'll get all sorts coming in looking for work. The good and the not so good.'

He was right. There were spoons missing, after we'd seen the first of three girls, tripping out of their Volvo, on spec. The next was dirty, and the third broke a plate.

None of them had been invited to call, but the word goes round. A big house, there had been a staff of seventy once. It flung a lot of girls on the job market when the old people went.

Sheenane had worked before, as a nurse. She rang up

to make an appointment, and we knew where she lived. It all seemed nice and safe.

'If only she didn't itch so much,' you objected, while we conferred in the pantry.

'That and the eyes,' I agreed, putting marmalade away. 'But she looks capable enough.'

So we took her on. Fifteen a day, extra for overtime. She was touchingly grateful, shaking my hand like a dog worrying a bone.

Hengist was never so affectionate. I knew it was him as soon as I heard the car. No-one except the itinerants would arrive with so much panache.

Whatever they did, they did with style. A trespassing boy with a cart of my wood had reined in a sprightly donkey and pre-empted my landlord's objections with a commentary on the weather.

They were like that, swift and elegant. You had your whip up to their goat, and they stepped in with a smile and a bunch of flowers. Probably your own flowers.

They were used to surviving in a bitter wilderness where all hands were against them. But their technique was the word as often as the sword.

They hung together, too, a flow of caravans with a bush telegraph and a common call to arms.

'Never strike one,' Harland advised me. 'Lay your hand on one, you're dead. They'll get you, some way.'

So I locked my temper up, when I heard the car. But I had my stick handy, on the window-sill. It pays to look vigilant.

Harland was behind me in the hall, polishing furniture, when I came out hospitably on the steps. He had the shotgun loaded across a dresser

There were three of them in the car. A middle-aged man with ginger hair got out, and then a swarthy, very handsome boy in his early teens. A woman stayed in the passenger seat, feeding a baby under a shawl.

72

'How are you?' the man said, it was never a question, while the boy was untying a rope that held the lid of the boot in place.

Then Hengist was up and out, a small mountain of flesh and fur, like a bear off a shield. Racing for a flock of sheep, a devouring angel.

The boy put his fingers in his mouth and let out a weird, sinewy whistle. The dog slithered to a halt, rounded, and began to shamble back towards the car.

You were there now, in your snake suit and a flying jacket, and you were in love with the dog already, I could see that. You were grinning the way a cat grins at cream.

'Very obedient animal,' the man was saying. 'He'll always come when you call.'

By now Hengist had reached the steps, and was laying his shaggy head against your thigh. He'd obviously been well-trained.

'Full of high spirits, too,' the man added.

The cats were now trooping into view, skirting an urn. When they saw Hengist, they stopped as one, and began to hiss.

Hengist frowned, no other word would do. Then he put his head on his paws, mournful as a lion on a monument.

'Forty pounds,' the man said flatly, his eyes beginning to flick away towards the trees.

I knew his feeling. They always seem too near when you're out there in the wind. You start to think about the available cover, and there isn't any.

'Make some tea, Liz,' I suggested, and we started to bargain.

I knew I could pay less in the twilight, they would grow nervous with darkness. But the afternoon was too young and bright.

I offered thirty, they asked if I wanted to sell any old

iron. Furniture, any chairs without legs or backs. They might take a look in the sheds.

But I knew the game. I didn't want them poking in the yard, finding the state of the defences.

They had a mug of tea on the steps, and we closed for thirty-five. Hengist lapped a saucer of milk, and he was one of the family. I couldn't resist him, any more than you could.

I watched the boy's eyes, amber fire. They licked at your calves, the architraves of the windows, the mute oils on the hall walls. I didn't like those eyes. They looked calculating.

But the man knew his manners.

'Good luck to the baby, lady,' he said, folding the notes away in his pocket.

'Yours, too,' I said, not to be outdone. 'These are hard times for a child.'

Then they were gone, rusted thunder and lightning scoring more potholes in my drive.

Hengist was a big eater. He made his way through a chicken carcase, opened his bowels on quarry tiles.

Harland was delighted with him.

'I'll see that he does his business in the yard,' he assured us. 'A good walk every evening, that's all he'll need.'

It was dark now, and the cats, both indoor and out, had gone about their ways. They were giving this hairy monster a wide berth.

'He'll weigh a few stone already,' Harland assessed, eyeing the guzzling bulk at its bowl. 'He'll be like a bull, when he's grown.'

Hengist lifted up his head, and gave vent to a howl. Not a bark, more of an eerie, quivering yell.

'Mountain hound,' said Harland, with satisfaction. 'That's his warning call. He's just showing you.'

Later, in the full darkness, we paced the boundaries,

74

just you and I. There was a great slew of stars, a full moon, racing through scattered cumulus.

You can feel safe on a night like that, ready to die. I might have said this, but I knew you wouldn't like it.

'Four weeks,' I said, instead. 'We have our things unpacked, most of them. A fire here and there. A maid and a dog.'

You snuggled against me, feeling the cold. No-one, I suppose, walks long at night in February. But I was enjoying the quietness, the distant view of the house, grey-lemon in the frosty light.

You were thinking of something else.

'Four weeks here, four months gone,' you said, laying my hand on your stomach.

'She'll be here in June,' I said. 'Irish like her mother.'

'I'm glad we don't know, though.'

I wasn't so sure. It seemed nice then to be looking forward to a son and heir, whatever I might say, diplomatically, about the chances of a daughter.

Then, ripping the night open, a quilt with a butcher's knife, there came a scream. A hare, maybe. I don't know. Quite near, outside the wall.

'Jesus Christ,' you said, sinking to your knees, a protective mound, head in, arms close.

'Nothing human,' I reassured you. 'It's all right. Really.'

But I wasn't sure. I bent, stroking your head, uncertain, a little frightened.

'It's not all right, you know,' you said, out of your mound. 'Even if it wasn't human, it's not all right. Not for whatever it was.'

You live in a wilderness, you fight to survive. What else is there? But I didn't say this.

'Let's go back in,' I suggested, feeling a spot of rain on my cheek. 'I'm feeling cold.'

Rain or blood, whatever it was. I wasn't cold, though I knew you were, shivering against my legs.

I helped you up, and we walked slowly towards the house, under Orion and facing the Plough. The rain thickened, hammering on our backs, and we walked faster.

Shaking drops off in the hall, I saw your face. Ravaged with pain.

'Indigestion,' you said. 'It's all right. The walk didn't really help.'

'I'm sorry.' I took you into my arms, holding you close.

There were times when the baby was hard to bear.

12

It doesn't bother me much any more. I suppose it's because I'm settled in. I even forget about it, most of the time.

I'm John Spencer, an old man with a young wife. I have a friend called Riley, an ex-wife called Linda. I live in the Earl's Court Road, or just off, after years in Ireland.

It begins in the Earl's Court Road, it all ends in the Earl's Court Road. You could say that, sometimes.

But it still nags. They used to say, you have a vision. You remember one of your earlier lives, the key one, and it solves your problems.

Not for me, it doesn't. It creates them. Pick up your pen to write a paragraph, it comes out in nine rhyming lines. Plan a chapter, it becomes a canto.

Could be worse, I suppose. At least it's not in Latin.

So I plug away at my prose, tell it the way it was. Write down the final solution, how to deal with the bastards.

Only they weren't the bastards. We were the bastards. That's the trouble. We did it first, all the way from King Henry.

I need a walk. I'm coughing more than I like. Smoke in the throat still, maybe.

That's how it ended. Will end, anyway. A start in smoke and an end in smoke. That's the way it was, you could say, when we first met, you and I.

You were down on your knees, holding a tray of pies, a savoury smell, smoke rising.

'Burned the buggers,' you were saying, then, seeing who I was, 'I'm so sorry.'

I didn't know who you might be, only saw how pretty you were.

'No,' I said, a bit rattled. 'It's me who ought to be sorry. I'm looking for the library. I must have opened the wrong door.'

'It's two along,' you said, then, smiling. 'You must be the speaker. I'm Ludowick's daughter. I'm doing the catering for your party, afterwards.'

'It smells great,' I said, staring at the burned pies.

A small kitchen, a great occasion. Light came through the stone mullions, a knife lay unused on the chopping-block. You knelt on the floor, the future I didn't even know I was waiting for.

'You're very generous,' you were saying. 'But I don't usually follow the King Alfred school of cookery.'

That's about all there was, until later. I left you clearing up the mess, and I went across the corridor and into the cosy, panelled room where I had to read.

We were miles north of the City, still inside the perimeter. Two years ago, Tom Gray had gone home, full of honours, and then in trouble. It's tough at the top.

He'd left me behind with a civil post, a legal appointment, lucrative enough. I had the lease on a property, enough leisure to be getting on with the great work they all expected of me.

I had my contacts. There were plums for the plucking, a certain amount of intellectual society. I knew your father before I even knew he had a daughter. He was writing well in those days and, what's better, I thought, rising fast.

So that when he invited me down for a few days, to stay and read, I was delighted.

'A few friends, John,' he suggested. 'A reading and

then a debate. We'll have some wine and cheese to finish the evening. Maybe a quiche or two, and a cake.'

I'd been down to Castle Talbot before, a defendable fortress, but one with an oriel window or two. A touch of comfort here and there.

So through the door and into the library I went.

A lean meeting, the seven deadly sins. Dark wood, a flare of lights here and there. Lamp at my elbow, where I would read, by the fire.

Briskett himself, on a crutch near the door, introducing me. Dark faces, cuff-links and cigar smoke. These were powerful men, clever enough to assess a rhyme, strong enough to break a neck.

'We all agree what the new regime demands,' your father began, swilling brandy in a rummer. 'Some idea of how to behave, a code hero, a rôle model. Could be a woman, yes, I agree. What with the energy lying where it does in Whitehall.'

'Drink to the lady,' someone said, in the darkness, and there was a clink and murmur for a moment.

'Man or a woman,' your father continued. 'Someone for the young to study and follow. Plenty of real people, of course. No problem there. But where's the theory? Where's the bible we can all point to and say, there's your manual.'

'Tasso,' someone said, from a window seat. 'It might have been him once.'

'Ariosto,' another voice replied, near the door.

'Italians, yes,' I hear your father replying. 'But where's the modern Ariosto? The definer of the gentleman in our own tongue?'

'Slow up, Ludo,' a slow drawl suggested. 'He's here in the room. Let him speak for himself.'

This was Long, the primate of Armagh. I'd know his boom in the pit of hell. Might hear it there, too, some would say.

He got a laugh while I cleared my throat. I looked out from the lit chamber of my page, a scorpion ringed with fire.

'Spencer,' your father was saying. 'The floor is yours.'

Of course, it wasn't. They interrupted a good deal. They were soldiers, politicians. They were used to a free exchange of ideas in private, and they didn't spare me. But I got the poem heard, some of it, and for the first time.

Strange to be reading what matters most to you in the world, and a woman's face blocking the words. Your blue eyes, and the hair dropping over your brow. They became the ivy round the fence of my page, the rhythm to the hard metre of morality.

'The problem is this,' I told them. 'How to combine the music with the message. We have to make English sing like Petrarch, but speak as clear as Machiavelli, and in favour of right against wrong.'

'But how?' gulped out a blunt voice, Dormer the lawyer's. A fat man who never let go of a bone of contention. Gluttony belching.

'Alliteration,' I suggested. 'A new stanza. Luck. Nobody knows.'

'Read us a little,' someone lisped. Sentleger, a dry soldier, with his anger always on a tight leash. I could hear him crunching paper into a ball. It set my teeth on edge.

You read, then. You take your life in your hands, get up in front of the five, or the four hundred. Lull them into your world with a joke, smash them open with imagery.

You know the score, Liz. You've seen it happen. The night you could hear a pin drop, Philip reading his wedding poem. A thousand hanging on his words, a stammer like the King's, perilously held in check.

Then there was Riley in Durham Castle, nine hundred

on the benches, a term paid for out of the takings. Hunched like a crow sheltering from the rain.

You were there. You know the way it can be. So imagine me in your father's darkness, weaving my own poor spell for the English rich, a powerful few. Laying the implacable cantos down, a carpet of gold for their prejudices to walk on.

'I see what you mean.'

That was Long, the voice of pride, an echo like a pruning-hook. Then Sentleger, welcome but meaningless. Taken in by the honey.

'Bloody good.'

The rest were divided. Some for the music, some for the puzzle interest. I came out and into the freezing corridor afterwards, drained and happy. The thing had been heard, the world alerted.

So then we were in the solar, a rattle of cold women and brilliant men, chandeliers, champagne.

I found you beside a platter of sausages, gathering wooden sticks in a saucer.

'I could hear them laughing,' you said. 'So it must have gone well.'

It's true. That's what you said. One has to say something.

'It didn't feel too funny,' I said. 'What with Sentleger and his whistle.'

That made you laugh. Make a girl laugh, you can make her do anything. I may even have risked saying that, I don't remember.

At any rate, there was sex in the air, that strange beautiful sense of knowing the other one wants it, too. Feeling sure of this. Tossing and lunging for it, while it's still all in words.

It was all in words then. It was in words for a long while. But I let the party rock to its own beat, a rack of the

81

boring and the ignorable, while I learned how close I could be to someone again.

'Talk to the famous,' you suggested once, after a while, as we perched on a rickety sofa. 'Dillon or Dormer.'

'Dillon's a prick. Dormer's an imbecile.'

You smiled, happy.

'You mean, you'd rather waste your time with me.'

'It looks like it.'

Later, I went to bed, in a room with a white bear. It must have been yours once. But the following morning you'd gone, back to school or away hunting.

That's how it all began. I rubbed the lamp, and a genie came out in a puff of smoke.

It was months, though, before we met again.

13

Why it took so long, I don't know. You were busy of course. But so was I. Buying and selling the lease of the manor. I had the place on the market for months, for my price.

Linda and the furniture, too. She wasn't easy there. I was in the middle of the whole business, money and emotion, when I saw you again.

Thought about you, of course. But you were in London, I was in Ireland. Then I was back in the Gate, and up at the Court, plotting with friends, hearing how you were.

You'd grown up, won a prize. I saw a picture of you in a magazine, with a wide hat and a smile. So I wrote you a letter, sent you a glove swathed in diamonds. What you will.

We met in a place to drink. A black October, and rain coming. Crowds round, a few whiskies. Then we were eating, somewhere else, out of doors, under an awning, despite the weather.

Until then, I don't know what we said. Something about your father, perhaps, the state of the nation. But now it was food for a time.

'Veal,' I suggested. 'The Italians are good on veal.' Good on everything, I might have added, remembering the manuals.

But I didn't. I was never coarse with you, ever. It seemed wrong, unnecessary.

'You like the Italians, don't you?'

The waiter hovering, the order taken. Wine in our glasses. Verdiccio, perhaps.

'Ariosto,' I agreed. 'He showed us the way.'

Ungaretti, I might have said. Ungaretti or Montale. The talk went through the years, looping and varying. You were a good listener, and you let me run.

I watched the gleam in your hair, torchlight on gold. Those Irish vowels, cut by a chin like an axe. You had one hand on a horse, the other on your bunsen burner. You seemed so young, so desirable.

'I'll work for the government,' you were saying. 'Be the Queen's lady. Three months here, and then I'm a girl in a white coat, with a phial of poison.'

You were that already, Liz. One drop of you, and I'd be away. I knew I would. I watched the shift of your figure under your clothes, a deliverance and a prison.

'I'm separated, yes.'

I must have told you before.

'I'm selling a house,' I said. 'I don't know what I'll do. Stay on in Ireland. Come home. I don't know.'

'Depends on the price?'

'Yes,' I said. 'It may depend on the price.'

You remember, Liz. I'm sure you do. A long look. A sort of long, sidelong look. The dessert there on the plates, a ruin of profiteroles. Unspoken futures pending.

Yes, I could buy another house. Yes, I could stay in Ireland. Yes, I could marry again.

Then you were dropping your eyes, drinking coffee. I felt my age, over a glass of brandy. Swilling fire in a bowl, playing with expectations.

Thirty years between us, thirty bloody years. Nothing could mount that pile of corpses with a Persian sword, opening the door to a fresh kingdom.

No, you say. Linda was there already, an odalisque on a divan. She was the obstacle, not the years.

But Linda was dying. Dying already, only an echo of

84

her gauzy veils. One push, and she was in the abyss. I swear it's true, Liz. It was true even then.

I walked you home, over the wet streets and the hint of winter. Not so far, a tingling twenty minutes.

'Come in for another coffee,' you said.

No, that won't have been then. That must have been later, the next time.

Goodnight, it must have been.

A kiss on the steps. Tongue in your lips, eel in a cave. The outriders of bliss.

There has to be sex, Liz. I told you this once, I don't know when. After a quarrel somewhere, your cheeks furrowed with tears. The terrible silence beginning. But I didn't need to speak. There always was the sex. There always is.

I remember the first time. A little room, with its cooker and postcards. A magnificent loaf, a narrow cot against the wall.

Stripping you, then. Stripping, yes, that lovely word. The outer layers of warm, forgettable things, a burden of laces and buttons.

Then the black skin of desire, the very words that stiffen.

'I don't usually do this.'

Down on your knees.

'Do it, I say. Do it now.

Dirty talk, loving thoughts. It happened so often.

'I have to go now.'

'Don't go. Please don't go. Stay a while.'

I did stay, for ever. But not then. There were voyages up to Lancashire, trips across the Irish Sea. The long shadow of Linda, you would say, staining everything. Weakening, perhaps, but still with power to spoil.

I began the sonnets, of course, earlier than you knew. But they were no good, then. Too much like those of

Philip's I'd seen, too much like anyone's. I was lost in my long poem, its endless repetition of twelves.

A last supper of a poem, you could say. A baker's dozen of books, waiting for the great lady's feast to round it off.

I took you to the zoo. Seeing the forlorn bears, up on their legs for bread, I thought of the Irish. Their clumsy intransigence. Their charming ways. That's how they seemed to me, in those days.

'We give them our stones and swords,' I told you. 'They bring us pancakes in return. It's all smiles for a while, and then they drop your porcelain on the flagstone.'

I was bitter, often. Seeing the way to power, and missing preferment. I wanted a mile of Ireland, space to ride from sea to sea, manors of my own, like Riley's. I could rule by the word, as he did by the sword. I knew the way.

You watched the war of feathers, ducks in an aviary. You saw how extreme I was.

'It's not so easy,' you said. 'They live by their own rules. You can't force them into another mould. You have to guide.'

Those were the days of Perrot's relaxations. They weren't working, so I believed. You want to decorate a room, you strip the old paper off. There's no other way.

I hated the bloodshed, but I liked the logic. You want to be understood, you clean the slate. Start from scratch.

'I was born there,' you were saying.

We walked arm in arm through the cages, the airy confines. Masters of beasts we could leave to die, or grant their food. Inferior creatures, delightful but primitive.

'I know the Irish people,' you told me. 'I even speak their language, a little. You judge them by ours, you miss the point in their lives.'

'I've read their poetry,' I replied. 'It may have grace,

but it lacks form. You need the classics for that, some discipline.'

'A Roman discipline,' you said, eyes on a hawk. 'Like a Roman road. There's more than one way through a bog.'

The snowy owl ruffled its feathers, the fish eagle spread its wings.

'The shortest distance between two points is a straight line.'

'The shortest, yes,' you said with a smile. 'But not always the nicest.'

Then you kissed me.

In your little room, we toasted fresh granary loaves, in the gardens at Kew, the sun shone on the Tree of Heaven. We talked about everything, our minds closing on each other like dogs on a fox.

In the Temperate House, it became your work's turn.

'It's a sort of infra-red,' you said, explaining an area of light. 'See in the dark, that sort of thing. It works by heat signals.'

I thought I could understand. I know better now.

There were maidenhair plants, shy at the warmth of a finger. It seemed so easy.

'We give out pulses,' I guessed. 'It picks them up, what you invent, and then translates them into an image. A photograph on a screen.'

'Sort of.'

'So the man in a car, an armoured car, say. An enemy armoured car. Could be drawn like a miniature on a dial. Every hair in place.'

'You're guessing.'

'Yes. But you'd know who he was. Could fix a laser in place, wipe him out.'

In the Tropical House, that made you laugh.

'Don't be so military,' you said, squeezing my arm. 'Think about earthquake victims. A woman, say. Under a fall of rock. Or a child in a pot-hole.'

I laughed with you.

'Besides,' you added, shaking a finger. 'It's classified.'

You were one of Burleigh's girls, a soldier of the Queen. What you did when you showed your pass and went through the gate was a mass of mystery, covered by the Official Secrets Act, even from the man you might one day marry.

But every night I went to your little room, I became your surrogate husband, the partaker in private of all you had to offer, official or public. It seemed very little to wait for, the secret of what you did on your bench, with the tubes.

I loved you, and you were mine. That was enough.

14

The message came after lunch. Brought by a boy on a bicycle, with a piercing whistle and a yo-yo. I don't know how he kept his balance.

'I'll have to speak about the gravel,' I told Harland, watching the boy negotiating the ruts.

A courier through no-man's land, raked by unseen eyes. Then he was ringing the bell, alive, and I held the flimsy orange in my hands.

'Nice place you have here,' the boy said, studying the view, lake and cows.

'Thank you.'

The usual curiosity, you have to satisfy it. Out of the womb they come, nosy as badgers, thrusting for information.

'Big for the two of you, though.'

'We'll be three soon,' I told him.

The boy laughed, a conniving laugh. A flight of starlings went up, off the grass, as if they were bits of his clothes, a black scattered cloak.

'No reply,' I said.

Then he was gone. I stood for a long time, pinching the envelope in my fingers, a dream message. Linda perhaps, wanting me back. Saying she had to have another operation. She had to see me.

But I knew who it was. Linda was in Brazil, it couldn't be her. It was Riley, somehow. It had to be.

I tore open the envelope, knowing before I read.

'See you at Lighthouse Road. Friday. Four, say.'

You were in the kitchen, managing Sheenane. She had the sink full of dirty water, crashing plates. Her skull's eyes were boring holes in the wall.

'Excuse me,' I said, hoping she would go.

But she didn't. She was too deep in her massacre of crockery.

'Sheenane,' you told her, seeing the point. 'Fetch the tray down, would you? It's in the hall, on the table.'

Hengist was in his huge basket, helping by panting. He came over and rubbed his fleas on my thigh, while Sheenane dried her hands, finger by finger. It took an age.

'She's hopeless,' you agreed, sensing my irritation when Sheenane finally went. 'She'll have to go.'

I was very jumpy, by then. You employ fools, you think you're being watched. They can't be so stupid. It must be some kind of disguise.

You put your lips up and kissed me on the chin. I felt the trembling slither down and coil in my stomach, out of sight.

'It's all right,' you said. 'She's gone now.'

Then I told you, nibbling a piece of shortbread. Sipping Ballygowan water. It all helps. I took a seat by the fire, feeding turf on, calming my hands, while I spoke.

'It can't be legal,' I said. 'I'd better go on my own. You'll be safe here with Harland.'

You were worried, though. I could see you were. You put your arm along Hengist's back, fondling the reassuring thickness of his fur.

'He's not at home,' I explained. 'It's a safe house.'

You were bitter, then. They were always barriers, the mutual secrets we tried not to share. Your military machines, my spies and earths.

'You mean I'm not supposed to know where it is.'

'Not really, no.'

The sun went in, and a long shadow struck through the room, laying darkness on our faces.

'I'll drive over after lunch. Be home in time for dinner.'

The way it was, I drove through town. Saw Sean in the street, ran the window down. He spoke with his back to the double gates, his yards away behind him.

'I've a matter to discuss, John,' he said, steadily. 'When you have some time, that is.'

I knew my Sean. This meant it was urgent, more or less. Probably more.

'Give me the gist,' I suggested.

Other cars went by, carts with logs and barrels. This was the new Ireland, all right. A man in green directing traffic, no-one obeying.

'It's the Desmonds again. They want a right of way.'

I spoke in rage, a twitching mist in my eyes.

'I'll be damned if I'll give them one.'

'Yes, well, we'd better talk. There are complications.'

I ran the window up, furious. Drove on, a flaming presence in blood and gold. None shall survive. Root out the croft and the byre. Let the ploughed fields run with gore.

Then I turned a switch in my mind. You have to, sometimes. Troubles never come singly. You do things one after another, you get them sorted out. You don't, you're a goner.

I thought about Riley. His coming back was a symbol, somehow. We were still a civilizing tower, maintaining our balance in a quagmire.

The Desmonds wanted me out. They wanted us all out. They wanted Riley in prison, dead even. It all hung together, in its own way.

I felt some comfort, thinking of Riley. Riley in Ireland, even Riley illegally in Ireland, made the world seem a safer place. More adventuresome perhaps, but safer.

Towards the end, you go down the hill towards

91

Youghal, following the bends of the river. You cross the bridges, watch the muddy banks where the tide has ebbed.

Here a pile of steaming dung, a donkey. There a dark face and a wave, over a spade. They look friendly. Always friendly.

But I drove expecting road blocks, a dead sheep or a stretch of rope. You have to be careful. You drive a Jaguar, you're the enemy, anywhere.

It's a fine bay, with a good harbour. This was where Riley cast his first anchor, brought his men ashore with their sacks of potatoes, their bales of tobacco leaves. You can almost smell the smoke in the air, on a calm day.

But this wasn't one. It began to rain, a sleety mean rain, when I hit the quay, coasting beside the derelict shacks, the handful of mansions.

Riley's house was up on the slope, near the old church, with a view of the sea. But he wasn't there. He was back on the run, barred from his pleasure gardens, his faultless acres.

Up in the woods, the weevils were in his trees, the weeds on his damp parterres. It was all empty, untenanted, while the law worked out the proprieties, and while Riley languished in prison.

Except that Riley was out, here. I turned the wipers on high. It was only a few hundred yards beyond the town, on the east cliff. I took the turn past the pub, and climbed fast.

I knew the way. We'd used the house before. But I drove past now, turned beyond the corner and came back on the other side. You never know. There might always be someone there before you. The wrong someone.

The rain was coming down hard. I got out, zipping my anorak to the neck. No sign of a car.

The house was one of a pair, the left half as you face the cliff, built into a hollow, facing straight out to the other promontory, across the water. A nice location, but the houses had been left alone.

Panes gone, a dodgy roof. I took the curl of stone steps to the front door.

Ringing the bell, I waited. Soaked to the skin already, beside a refractory palm. A surreal, science-fiction thing in the rain.

Then he was there. The usual minder, slapping my pockets for a gun. I was over the threshold, examining the unchanged, still peeling paperwork in the hall. Roses on what was once a cream ground.

Riley was upstairs. The minder led the way, sure of me now, past the half landing with its shit-orange shower-room, his fingers playing with the banisters. A lover of Georgian turning, I thought irrelevantly. You find them everywhere.

It hadn't changed, that familiar room. The double doors to the balcony, the recess towards the kitchen, that incongruous Edwardian mantel over the fire.

Riley was in the alcove, on the window-seat. He got up when I came in, and my heart turned over, he looked so tired.

'Hello, old lad,' he said.

You could never convey Riley. He was too much a balance of opposites, a blend of the rock and the wind. The pictures all show him with his little dagger of a beard, and a fancy collar, usually.

But I remember him clean-shaven more often, as he was now, and in combat gear. Dull and casual.

'You've been travelling,' he said. 'Let me offer you tea. Roger, tea.'

The minder went into the kitchen, and Riley motioned for me to sit in the window, facing him. He seemed less tired now, as if the fact of my arrival was filling him up like a tap with energy. It was a flattering thought, very typical of Riley and his charm. He could always make you feel that he needed you. Still can, for that matter.

'You're out on bail,' I suggested, watching the sleet drawn like a shower-curtain over the sea.

'Skipped, yes.'

Riley smiled, a bizarre rictus. When he smiles it's like a tiger, at feeding-time.

'The bail was easy. The skipping, less so. I had to borrow a vessel. Bit of help from the Special Service there.'

He turned his mouth down, mock-glum.

'I'm afraid that meant Roger.'

You know Riley, you stop wondering how the British Army can land a man by sea in a foreign country.

'No visa, I'm afraid. So I can't run over to see Liz. How is she, the old slag?'

'She's great, Riley. Sends you her love.'

Then I paused, wondering if I should risk what he knew I would risk.

'How's Liz?'

Riley laughed, and we put our palms forward and slapped hands. We were like two children, we'd never got over both having wives with the same name. But Riley's marriage had never been easy, it was part of the reason he was where he was.

'She's OK, John. It's working out.'

Then the tea was in, on a small spindly table with a strip of linoleum for a cloth. Riley had a taste for civilization, and Roger, it seemed, was able to mash tea.

'Your buns?' I asked him, biting into a very palatable fairy cake.

'I did bake them, yes.'

The sleazy furniture, and this great magnate, one of the richest men of our time. A hired killer, who was a virtuoso with an oven. Contrasts and comparisons, the stuff of farce.

94

Then Riley came to the point.

'It's not just a social call,' he said. 'I'm here on business. Take a look at the green-houses. Make sure the flowers are watered.'

I had a sense that he meant this literally as well as metaphorically. But I didn't ask. He was a careful man and he liked to come round to his message in his own time.

'Have another bun.'

'Thanks.'

'We'll go round the back for this one. You never know when they're watching.'

I didn't ask him who. I followed through to the stale bedroom, a squalid box with its pair of windows backed on the streaming rock. There was water dancing off the edges of stones, climbing trees. It was like being in a cave.

I remembered other times in this nasty room, other minders with harder work than baking buns. But Riley was sensitive to this.

'I won't keep you, John. It's not a room I like myself. But it's dead secure.'

Riley stared out at the rain.

'There's going to be trouble,' he said, slowly. 'Don't ask me how I know, but I do. O'Neill has plans for a take-over bid. You know what I mean, I imagine?'

I nodded. I did know.

'So you see, there'll be knock-on effects. The Desmonds, for instance. They'll want a piece of the pie.'

'It's not altogether a surprise,' I said. 'I've had some hints.'

Riley turned and looked at me.

'John,' he said. 'It's going to get worse. You may have to fight for what you own. That's what I came here to tell you. I wanted you to hear it directly from me. It's not a cheerful message, but it's true.'

There were stains on the wall I saw now, blood or pus.

No-one had given instructions for a sanitation job. You stand in the torture chamber, you hear some nasty news.

'I have to go home,' Riley said. 'I'll see you soon. Don't worry, I'll be back.'

I shook hand with him.

'I'll finish *Cynthia* one day,' he was saying, walking down the stairs with me. 'Can't let you have it all your own way with the old lady.'

Then he was checking the hall, motioning Roger to open the door.

'I wish we had time to talk about your new poems,' Riley said. 'After all, they're what we're fighting for.'

Then I was out in the rain, running for the car.

15

About then, it all began to tie in. The car, first. You drive something that fine, you get no trouble. Usually, I mean.

It must have been north of Mallow somewhere I stopped for petrol. Watching the clouds gather again while they filled both tanks.

'Rotten weather.'

'Aye.'

I paid my dues, conversation, money. Then I was back in the driving-seat, flicking the starter.

No go, not a spark. A mule with its heels dug in. I was out in the road, feeling the cold wind, easing the bonnet open.

You bugger, I'm thinking. You dare do this to me.

But it never does. I was checking the plugs for water, tapping the alternator.

'Battery, maybe.'

The man who had filled me up had a knotty face. Cheeks like a bunch of grapes. A drinker.

'Pull over,' he suggested. 'We'll take a look in the workshop.'

Well, it wasn't pull over, it was push. But he gave me a hand, rain flailing now.

I had some tea in the town. Charleyville, that's where it was. One street of French elegance, and a bridge of ruins. They're all the same. A mill and the castle down, then the bourgeois rampant.

I tried to telephone, was worried when I had no answer. Well, it was early. But it wasn't, really.

Six o'clock. Then eight, then nine. Still no answer. I'd had my dinner by then, some mince and a black forest gâteau. I'd been to and fro to the workshop, and they had the starter motor out on the floor. In pieces.

'We'll work late for you. Finish the job.'

A grinning boy, and the brother of grape-face.

You get a favour done, you have to sit still and wait. I was jumpy, though. You couldn't be out. No answer meant you were in, but not hearing. I didn't know why.

I tried reading the magazines in The Imperial Hotel. Old farming journals, a copy of the local newspaper. Couples about to marry, someone with a prize pumpkin.

Ten or eleven, they finished. Wrote out their astronomical bill, accepted my very irritated thanks. I was on my way.

By then, I was too worried to wonder why it had happened. Why there. Why they had stayed so late, not said we'll do it tomorrow, we'll hire you a car.

Well, they were nice people. You get some. I wonder. These nice people had cost me six hours. I got home after two.

A badger crossed the path. You get some. I took it very slowly, through the trees. I didn't want to land in the ditch.

No lights on, a bad sign. I had the car door open, keys jangling, listening. Total silence.

Then I was through the door, the fortress around me. Safety in darkness, maybe. These are the walls I know. Domestic spirits, help me.

'Liz,' I called. 'It's me.'

No answer. I went up the stairs fast, arm over arm on the rail. The limp slows me.

The bedroom door was locked. I shook the handle. You must have the bar across.

'Liz,' I called. 'Let me in.'

Then the merciful sound of the bolt running. I was through, in the big room.

You were fully dressed. A bottle of sherry on a small table beside you, near the fire. But you weren't drinking now, not since the baby.

Incongruous detail, sweet Jesus Christ, one of my swords on the chest of drawers.

It took a while. You let go when I came in. There were tears and shaking a long time, before you could speak. Then it flowed out, the whole story.

'I came to bed early,' you told me. 'I meant to read, I suppose. But I fell asleep.'

'I telephoned,' I told you. 'I telephoned, several times.'

You shook your head.

'I didn't hear. I don't know. Maybe the lines are down.'

Well, they were down before. It happens. But the same day the lines are down and the car won't start, you feel the pressure. I did then.

'Go on,' I said.

You had a comb in your hair, some tortoiseshell. You took it out, letting the gold onto your shoulders. Antlers of flame in the grate. The fire arched from the hearth to your neck.

'Something woke me. I don't know what. I was in a confused dream. Then I was wide awake, hearing the sound of hooves, animals moving. I thought it was Harland at first, with the ponies.'

I poured some sherry, into your glass. Drank it, listening hard.

'I heard a crash, then another. Breaking glass. I felt angry at first, very angry. I thought he was being careless, had let them smash something.'

You smiled at me, wanly.

'I don't think I really knew what time it was. I put on

99

my dressing-gown, went downstairs to the back door and switched the outside light on.'

You covered your face with your hands, shuddering. I took you by the hand, lifted you over, baby and all, hoisted you onto my lap, and the baby moved, I'll swear.

'Go on,' I said softly. 'It's all right.'

'I opened the door, wide, they were there. About fifty of them, coming into the yard from the back gate. As if they were being poured from a jug, out of the darkness.'

I was hugging you tight, you were shivering.

'Get into bed,' I said. 'You'll be warm there.'

You did as I told you, then stared up at me from the pillow, eyes flecks of ice.

'They were twenty yards away, John, and an old one, a really big one, came hell for leather for me with his horns down. Straight for the door.'

'You got it closed,' I told you. 'Somehow you got it barred, in time.'

'Go downstairs. Take a look for yourself.'

They were gone, of course. But the yard was a shambles. Broken glass everywhere from windows they'd smashed, saplings uprooted and shrubs ripped from their beds. Walls flecked with blood where they'd gored each other.

They do a lot of harm with their horns, when they're frightened.

That's what Harland told me once, when we nudged through a herd of them, in the car. Their shoulders above our heads, pizzles reeking beyond the windows. Boned skulls, a rattle of staves on the metal.

I walked through a slaughterhouse, the stink of their calling-cards in my nostrils. Piles of dung it would take us weeks to clear.

Then I went back in, by the door the bull had charged. A panel had splintered, rammed, as if by a sword.

'I swear there were dogs,' you told me later. 'Dogs

100

herding them in. I'll not say men, there was too much noise to tell. But I heard horses neighing.'

We got some sleep, not much. It was a dry, fresh morning, and I took Harland with me, briefing him first. He wasn't hopeful, but he came.

Jimmy Desmond's place was a shack like a beached caravan. Two rooms, and a bath in the kitchen.

He came to the door, a gnarled seventy year old, with braces over his bare shoulders. Hair like ivory.

I didn't like the way he smiled, and he got his blow in first.

'Forget about the fence,' he told me, waving his hand. 'Think nothing of it now. The beasts are all back in their field.'

I could see them over his shoulder, a peaceful, grazing block of evil. But when the oestrus seethes in their bowels, then beware.

'You know the law, Jimmy,' Harland reminded him, bleak as a knife. 'If the stakes are down, it's your responsibility. Wire, too.'

Breed up a pair of sea lawyers, you pick up a subterfuge yourself. He scratched his arm while he answered.

'I wonder, now. We'd have to be seeing what the courts would say. You see, I believe a gate may have been left open. A bit of carelessness on somebody's part.'

I saw red then. A sky of blood, pipes running with gore. Vengeance and ecstasy.

'You damned scoundrel,' I said. 'You drove the cattle in. You and your bloody sons. You've wrecked my property. You frightened the life out of my wife. You nearly killed her. I'll see you in prison for this.'

He said nothing. Then he spat on the ground.

'That's not the law talking, Spencer,' he said. 'You'd better see your solicitor. You may have to eat your words.'

I let Harland drive me home, recovering in the passenger seat.

101

'You may be right,' he told me, negotiating the puddles. 'O'Neill has a garage in Charleyville, they could interfere with your car. He has friends in the telephone business, too, they might doctor your lines. I don't know. But you can't prove anything.'

We came to a halt for a moment, hazelnut catkins overhanging the car. A tractor went by, a smiling face. Paul Desmond's.

'Bullocks do escape,' Harland said. 'It's happened before. It might be an accident.'

'Liz heard their horses. She saw dogs.'

But I knew his answer, before he gave it.

'Forgive me, John. You know what the courts will say. There were no witnesses. She was frightened, yes. Pregnant women imagine strange things sometimes. Especially, when their husbands are away from home. Who ought to be there looking after them.'

The house was in sight now.

'Hengist,' I said. 'He didn't even bark. They must have doped his food.'

You live with paranoia, it starts to fit the facts. But there was a car in front of the house, and this distracted me.

A blue car, with a light on the roof.

'It's the garda,' Harland said.

16

He was in plain clothes, of course. You had him pinned in the drawing-room, with a cup of coffee. Saloon, or whatever. Drinking sack, an off-duty call.

The police come in, you can paint your own room, study or cell. It's all the same, you're on trial, swear what you will.

The man got up when he heard me, a smile under a black moustache, legacy of the Tans. I could see my face in his shoes.

'A fine old place this,' he was saying, gesturing round at the plasterwork.

I went round and stood behind your chair, my arm on your shoulder. Spanish leather under my fingers, cold as lizard-skin.

'Italian craftsmen,' I told him. 'But the labour was Irish.'

Overhead the great fans in the ceiling curled in their crispness, the beams glittered with new paint. I could see Harland through the window, parking the car.

'The same old story, eh? A foreign lead, a local following.'

We all laughed, three good friends on a sunny morning enjoying their coffee together.

'Have another biscuit,' you suggested, handing him a box, the Queen's face on the lid, the rainbow portrait.

He took a couple, munching into a comfortable silence. But I felt it bristle, like the back of a porcupine.

'So you're settling in, John.'

He managed to give this opinion a threatening emphasis, an ambiguous resonance. But I wasn't going to help him. I took a seat on a pink lady's-chair, staring up at the cornucopia above the fire.

'Good to be back,' I said.

Then he began to make his effort, seeing he had to lead the way.

'We need men like you,' he said, laying his cup on the floor. 'Sensible men who remember the past, who want to help with the future.'

He wiped crumbs from his mouth.

'Things have changed,' he stressed. 'It has to be hand in hand from now on.'

He'd been with the force in the occupation, out on the beat with his gun and truncheon. Swap his grey tweeds for a green jacket, there he was. Agent of ours, collaborator for the kill.

I watched him running down like a clockwork doll.

'We both know what I mean, John. There have to be fresh alliances, new liaisons. A bit of give and take.'

Here it comes, I was thinking.

'Old contacts, for instance. Old friends. One may have to weigh their benefits.'

I let his pause go on and on.

'I'll make some more coffee,' you said, rising.

But, no. He held up his hand, like a man stopping traffic.

'I've had enough,' he said.

Then I stood up, leaning on the mantelpiece, looking down.

'I saw Riley yesterday,' I said. 'Over in Youghal, on holiday.'

'I know, John. That's why I'm here.'

A handkerchief in his top pocket, a little white mountain. Hooded eyes, like a hawk's. The might of the guards.

'The trouble with Riley is, he was careless about his visa.'

'Could happen to anyone.'

Why am I talking? Why am I saying this? Dear Jesus Christ.

'Of course. To you or me, even. The trouble with Riley is, he came in with some friends. From the Special Boat Squadron.'

He was brushing something off his trousers, looking ready to go. They always do before the climax.

'We neither of us want any trouble, the police over there and ourselves. We co-operate. Men like Riley – men like O'Neill, too, I'm not pussy-footing – they're out of date. They make waves. I want a calm Ireland, a place where you and I can smoke and be real friends. I'm not concerned with rights and wrongs. I don't want men here whom other men want to kill. That's all.'

He was on his feet now, a stocky presence with a pistol out of sight under his arm.

'I like Riley,' he said, easily. 'He's a kind of genius, in his way. But I'd rather you didn't see him again, if he gets back in touch. Or let me know first, at any rate. I just don't want any trouble.'

I walked with him to the door.

'Let me know if there's any way I can help you,' he said. 'Any little problems you have, while you're here.'

I wanted to mention the railings, the bullocks, but it wasn't the time.

'I will,' I said.

Then you were out on the steps beside me, and we were strolling down a cattle ditch, bending to inspect a bright fungus, hundreds of them like broken china, brown on the outside of the cups, blood in the bowl.

'Never saw any of these before,' you said.

'Nor I.'

'The police followed you,' you said. 'You led them to Riley, that's what you think.'

'I hope not,' I said, refusing to accept the idea. 'I don't know. It's possible.'

Poison was on the ground, scattered everywhere, in the air. A dead stoat, hanging from a tree.

You go on the best you can, you come out the other side. I hope.

Sometimes it all seems written down, like in a script. The actions lock into the words, out ahead of them like shadows before the sun. What can you do?

Then I saw your face, white and drawn.

'He's kicking me in the groin,' you said, wincing.

But this was the world we lived in now, where the child fought to be born, ready with fists and feet for the enemy waiting.

17

I went by the Underground, strap-hung amongst the mob, the plebeian young. Nobody gave me a seat.

Nine stops, and a flight of stairs, an escalator. Leaning on the torn mesh of the rail, eyeing the girls going down. Skirts on the other side, a wash of crackling.

Funny the way it stirs you, seeing them slide away, going out and under. Thighs like the years, dark and slippery. White and soft.

You see all of England, the way she is now, on the moving stairs. Those going up, running, or resting for another effort. Those going down, faces blackened with soot or tears.

I came up out of the dark, ignoring the advertising, placarding lust and fear. Shouldering into the light, through women dressed in La Perla girdles under their frocks, men with zippered horns. London rampant, the phantasmagoria of sex.

You stroll down Piccadilly, you find a man begging in the road. I had my cane in a cap of coins, gave him another, what used to be called a florin.

Bugger all, would buy him a cigarette. So he gave me the two finger sign. I don't blame him.

'Up yours, squire.'

'I'm sorry, I didn't think. I've been away.'

Then it was gold, apologizing. A sovereign for thy pains, fellow.

Then it was passing the new church, the old sandwich bar. A man selling Standards, from a barrow. Jesus, if only we could. Sell Standards, I mean. They'd all be models, the strap hangers behind their paper nudes.

I stopped for a rest. Saw the headline on the hoarding. England's twenty-first. Opening dates for the north bank exhibition, the new century's.

A young man going out for a swim, a key embroidered on his trunks. The key of the door. A topless girl with a key-hole on her briefs. The mating years. I see them one more time I'll spew.

Into the square, through the double doors. I had to leave my coat and my cane. You live in the shadow of all those books, you see more old men than you do in Florida. I felt safer suddenly, more fit, more virile.

The clock on three, the great files creaking in their bindings. Lousy dust jackets from lousier novels up on the boards. I felt at home.

Ascend the stairs, that whirl of mahogany to the woman's loo. Never been in there. Never will, I suppose.

You get forgetful, though, they take your ticket away. It happens. Friend of a friend, yes.

I remember Conquest at seventy, here on the stairs. Showing me the miniature of his latest wife, his third. Lovely beyond the dreams of adolescence.

'One for the road, eh?'

Smiling. As one might smile before the guns. The noose. The grip in the groin.

I took it easy into the stacks, ran the lights on by their cords. Flooding scholars in dingy alcoves. Wenches with skirts up to their thighs.

I found the rack, slid my fingers over the yielding spines. Had what I wanted out in three seconds.

Then it was over to a table, a rare monkish corner filtering sun. Flipping the pages over, the batters the colour of horn.

I started to read. I mean, you could start a book there, 'I started to read.'

108

They don't matter, the facts, the words. He was born in London, yes. Edmund, not John. Educated at Cambridge, yes. But middle class, that's the comparison. A man rising.

Came from the north, though. Made influential friends. The question is why. Why Ireland. Why there. Why then.

You sit on a bentwood chair by an open window, the world is all why. There are no answers there, only the lilting queries, the tilting blocks of leaves.

I was interested for years. I began reading in England, stopped with the fourth canto. Linda was there, big with Sylvanus. I had to anticipate him, used the Queen for a model, a kind of melody. I wrote a poem.

That doesn't make me be him. It makes me like him, yes. It makes me like him a lot.

He became a friend of Philip's, formed his style. Broke free. The movements come and you ride their backs. I did myself, I agree.

It's not a court of law, I don't have to say this. I'm not on a couch. I went to the priest, and he failed me.

He went north. He met his first wife. She refused him. They fell in love, they lived together for years. She left him. He didn't want her to. He never forgot her.

But you get over things, Liz. You do forget. He did forget. He married again.

They owned a big house in Ireland, a castle with many acres. Furnished the land with their flowers, the lake with their birds.

I read all that. I made notes. I explained it all to myself, cold in the sun. Surrounded by other writers, close to other writers they knew and loved, whom they might almost have been themselves, but they weren't. Surrounded by words, in a world of books.

It isn't, though. Out here it's a world of real people, who choose what we do. It's not what's written that counts. It's what we write.

109

I put the biography back on the shelf. I took the stairs with my hand on the rail. Passing photographs of the famous, the forgotten dead.

I saw a man I once shook hands with, on the wall. I talked with a man I once gave work to, in the hall.

Then I was out in the air. I took a bus, riding high over streets paved with sweat and ribbons.

He never did this. He was on a horse, yes, in the Mall. He saw the cherry blossom foam on the trees. Petticoats in a bordello.

I rode out ahead, racing beyond the pen trailing. I felt the wind and the cold, I enjoyed the sense of being alive. I even bought a ticket, with the right money.

Then I was here, in the square. I walked through buskers and apple-sellers. I got you a bunch of daffodils, and some soap, and a magazine.

I came upstairs with them all in my arms. I took my time. I thought you might not be home yet, still away with your sister, shopping.

Here I am, Liz. It makes me happy to find you here, after all. Rising clean from your tiny work at the white table, ruins of coffee composing themselves on a steel tray by your side.

You see, it's you and me. Not him and her, as I used to think. We have a chance.

'Lie down on the bed, hold me close to you.'

'You're trembling.'

'I want to make love to you.'

'Don't be silly, you've still got your coat on.'

'Forget my coat.'

Pornography seeping through from the text, life rising out of her torpor, nude with desire.

They lay in the bower of bliss, under eglantine and ivy. He drank the ambergris from beneath her nether lips, making her quiver with joy.

Yes, but I do the same. But you do the same.

110

So mount me, Liz. Open thy jerkin, wench.

The words, the words. They make me want to come. They lead the way.

He never did this. He can't have done. I won't have it, I won't.

I want to come.

Stop me, John. Stop me, Edmund. Stop me.

Sweet Thames another time run softly till I end my song.

18

'I can't go on,' you said.

I don't know when it was. We were in the service kitchen, a chopped wedge off a corridor, crouching over a gas fire. A blaze of turf, whatever.

It wasn't the bullocks. Or the guard. They weren't the last straw. You were two months from the gates of birth, and the pressure was on.

I see you now in your grey angora cardigan, a shapeless cloud. Your face drawn like a hatchet out of the fur. But you wouldn't have worn it, ever, without the child.

'I'm tired of it,' you said.

I heard the wall clock, it had moved in with us for warmth, hesitating in its stride. You listen to them regularly, they seem to be warning you. I'm going to stop. But they never do.

Not if they're straight on the wall. Not if they hang right. They go on until they die.

I put my hand on your wrist, feeling the pulse. It was deep and sound. I put my head in the crook of your neck, not knowing what to do.

I was cold. We both were. Two bars of gas, though, I was feeling generous. The bulbs burned in their sockets, clean and still under their shades. Pregnant women, legless, beneath wide skirts.

'I'll ring Rogers,' I said, frustrated. 'He may be able to prescribe something.'

But it wasn't the baby. The baby was always there, the iron soldier in the womb, the background.

The baby would come in its own time, and the pressure would still be there. It was Linda, that was the trouble. Reaching out of the telephone. Out of the mail bag like a dead hand from the sea.

'I can't bear it any more,' you said.

There was mist on the window, coffee cold on the flushed chenille.

I kissed your cheek, feeling it stiff, and I tried to be calm. Tried to be sure.

I'd driven over the back of Ireland to the capital, alone. You hadn't wanted to come, and I hadn't forced you.

The letter had risen on spider's legs, out of a slew of bills. Ossian wheezing over a slab of cake in the hall. A fat man, and a curious one.

'Good news, John,' he suggested, watching me paint a smile on my face.

But you were staring into your plate. You knew what it was. Asthmatic Ossian, with his little brown cigars and his eyes like paper-knives. He could only guess.

'I've won a prize,' I told him. 'Two weeks in the bogside with Charlie.'

Or maybe Bonnie Prince Charlie. Or Tom Gray or Hugh O'Neill. We shared a hatred of all politicians, and I liked to see him laugh. It took the curse off his heavy breathing.

So he was gone, with his crumbs and his cream, and there we were. You sick, I reading.

'She's in Dublin next Tuesday,' I said. 'Recording for *Nightwatch* in the Flood Street studios. She wants us both to go up and see her. Dinner, maybe, she says.'

'You'd better go,' you said, stone-hard.

Then you went through the front door, knelt on the terrace, ripping at weeds. I followed you, saw your hands, bloody already.

'Come,' I said, kneeling beside you. 'Please come.'

But, no. You wouldn't. So I went alone. A big so, I now saw. But I'd felt I had to, when the letter came.

My son, Sylvanus, how was he. The agreement about the furniture. There were so many things unsettled. I had to keep channels open. So I thought.

So I drove in a storm of freak hail, the little balls lashing on the windscreen. White and hard, they could kill a tit. Or blind a cow, maybe, one in the eye.

The towns rolled by, all the same in the crowded air. It was weather I drove through, not architecture. The chain that held me unreeling out of your body at every mile, a tug of guilt.

I have to go, I told myself. It's only civil. She means nothing now.

Then she was there, a face through glass. I was in the control room, hands all round me doing things to switches, potentiometers. The rigid paraphernalia of a media exercise, people and machines.

I shook the drops off my coat, remembered the car safely parked on a bomb-site. Your hand waving from the doorway in the last sun before the hail.

She was older, of course. A sort of tricorne hat on her long hair, where the first streaks of grey had come. That face like a Benin mask, inscrutably dour.

There had been a time. Yes, there had been a time. But now it was far away, and I lived outside her, a tree on another planet.

I watched her doing the things she was good at. Answering questions, moving her thin serious hands. She had a cigarette in an ash tray, and she picked it up, and sucked the smoke in, leaning her head back, the way she had always done.

Then she saw me. An alien fish in a distant aquarium. Remote and melancholy. But she smiled, an instant flash of the old pleasure crossing her face. Delighted, it seemed, to know I was still there, although no longer close. Or dangerous.

After the programme, we sat with tea in a canteen.

Imagine the lutes and dulcimers. Those Yorkshire suitors with their slow pavanes. It was never so. But I remember it so, as if it was.

'He's well,' she told me, about Sylvanus. 'A boy now, you know. You would hardly recognize him.'

She nibbled an egg sandwich, nodding to passing technicians who stared a bit longer than they might have done. The famous face from the papers, the name on the screen.

Someone even came over, brasher than most, and asked for her autograph.

'You should ask for his,' she told the girl, as she signed. 'He's a famous poet.'

Aye, and in all the anthologies. In the English Men of Letters series, my name in blue on the beige, my life all written down by the Dean of St Paul's.

But the girl only smiled. She thought it must be a joke. Her hero was being gracious to this elderly farmer with the limp and the cane.

'Let's go,' Linda said. 'We'll have nothing but interruptions here.'

We resumed in a gloomy bar, miles underground, with Guinness on mats, and a bowl of potato crisps. It was still Sylvanus, news of the flesh, for a time.

'He plays a lot of soccer,' Linda said. 'He has your temper.'

I thought of my son as if painted on enamel, encased in her dream. Serving out his life sentence in a cage I couldn't reach. But I liked to think of my vices, imprisoned under his skin, struggling to work free.

'Give him my love,' I suggested, sombrely.

Linda had not lost her reticence. She had something to say, at the front of her mind, I knew. But she kept it there. Discussing films, the parts she could have. The market value of oil shares.

She had money in stock now, it seemed. Was out of

115

property and into the fluctuations of microchips. I heard her offering tips, moving the base of my glass in a pool of froth.

It was late, later than I wanted. There would have to be dinner soon, if we didn't go. I would have to drive in the dark, worrying.

Then it came out, what had always been there, waiting. Its face all innocence, but it would break us.

'I want to see your new poem,' Linda said. 'I hear it's a masterpiece.'

I was shaken, surprised. She'd never taken much notice of what I wrote. It didn't make us money, and few of her friends could read. Figures were fine, of course, in *Spotlight*, or a balance sheet. But not the mathematics of metre.

'I met Riley one day,' she was saying. 'We had a steak at The Duck. He said your poem, what he'd seen of it, was the best we have. He said there was no-one else in English in sight of you. He thought the Queen would make you laureate, when Hilary dies.'

'Hilary's ill,' I said, involuntarily.

'It means a position, a pension for you.'

He was dying of cancer, people said. Might have only a few months to live.

A man came past the table, squinting at Linda as if she was a menu. But she only smiled. She was smiling more than she used to.

'Show me the poem,' Linda said. 'I can get it published. Riley and I between us. We'll make you famous. I owe you that.'

I remembered the years intriguing with agents, addressing letters to impresarios. Yes, I had helped her. I wanted to. But she was right, there was a debt to pay, and she had connections. Between them, she and Riley could make my name.

'Show me the poem,' Linda insisted. 'Send me a copy, in London.'

116

Then I had crossed the Rubicon, and was where I could never get back from. It seemed so simple then, but it wasn't.

'All right,' I said. 'I will. Thank you.'

I don't know what her motives were. Perhaps she felt, at first, there was really a debt of honour, and wanted to pay me back. Or perhaps she thought, and this was my cynicism, her part in the publication would add to her own fame. I can't believe, at that stage, she knew where she really meant to go. It would break my heart.

So Linda was on her feet. Arranging her silks, draining her glass.

'You'll have to start,' she said. 'I know you won't want to be late for dinner. Give Liz my love.'

It seemed a touch of affection, at the time. Not wanting to separate us, realizing my pull to the west.

You saw it differently, though, when I reached the house at nine. The twilight in its pool of ink. The last of the crows dwindling into their tangled roosts.

'I didn't wait,' you said, uncompromisingly. 'There's a bit of ham, and some soup I could heat.'

I gave you the afternoon, blow by blow. Awkward over a sweet martini, while you were sewing.

'She means well,' I suggested. 'I really think she means well.'

But you were adamant, thrusting your needle through bare hessian. Moulding a shield, your family's arms, on the baby's quilt.

'So you settled about the furniture,' you said.

'Well, no. You see.'

But there was no You see. It hadn't been mentioned. The way you saw it, I'd failed. Worse, I'd let you down. I'd wasted an afternoon in idle chat with my former wife, whom you hated.

'I'm sorry,' I said, and I was sincere. 'I really am. I make

117

the mistake of always wanting to seem polite. I wouldn't have hurt you for any reward, and I have done. I'm sorry.'

But you wouldn't be comforted. You didn't want Linda anywhere near me. Near my body or near my poem.

'Don't write to her,' you said. 'She'll do us some harm, I know she will.'

I didn't believe you. I went out, and down to the kitchen, and made myself a sandwich. Fed the cats a plate of old kidneys, and fondled Hengist, as he lay in his basket.

I felt the lust of fame, and I thought Linda could help. I was wrong, Liz, and you were right. Forgive me.

19

I don't know when he came over first. Riley, I mean. It must have been after the Falklands, the days of the great armada. I seem to remember him always in uniform, a sailor's oaths on his lips.

But it wasn't so. He had Smerwick, too, and those bodies in the barn to share with me. There was land violence as well as water victory between us. That fleck of blood on his arm.

You know a hero, you don't go over the history of torture. We kept quiet, I suppose. We buried our dead. It was more fun to share verse than nightmares.

But the nightmares were there. I put more than one occasion together, but I always seemed to meet Riley under a blackening shadow. Men in armour clearing a field of fire.

So I sit on the steps. A warm day in the eighties, cherry laurel out in the wood. It must have been April.

I hear the skirl of the engine first, see the dry khaki a minute later. A green star, a clamp of iron over the sun.

Then it was overhead, hammering the blood out of the clouds, a gun-ship circling. Articulated legs coming down to make their grip on the lawn. Everything under a darkening coldness.

I went forward, over the terrace, down from the ramparts. Towards the distinguished visitor. The door in the monster hanging open already to let him through.

But the soldiers came first. The Republican guard with their automatic weapons, covering the lake and the trees.

Then the ladder was down, and here was Riley, neat in his British combat gear, a foreign general.

He still had his beard then, and a patch over one eye. A splinter of mail from a shell, the Belgrano's perhaps.

We shook hands, happy to see each other. We must have been because we always were, whatever was due to come.

Then he thanked the young soldier who had followed him down with a couple of bags. Waved with a sort of ironic elegance to the pilot, and watched the helicopter thunder upwards and bank away.

I noticed the four men at arms who were still on the ground. Saw them disappear in a clump of bushes at the edge of the field.

'Sorry about the pizazz.'

I smiled. You see Riley, you buy what he brings. I knew that then. But he looked apologetic, and he wasn't smiling himself.

'They insisted,' he said. 'It seems I'm a high risk import. They don't want some nutter putting a ball in my guts. It would spoil the honeymoon with Westminster if they sent me back in a coffin.'

But you were there now, dazzling in polka dots and straw. Suppose you were. You often were. You liked Riley, before you learned what trouble he used to bring.

'Whiskey, Riley,' you said, handing him a full glass. 'Then I'll leave you two for the all-boys-together session.'

'Superb. Superb.'

He said it twice, making it clear he didn't mean the whiskey. Finger-tips at his lips in a parody of Italian love-making.

But he let you go. He has that rare flair for flattering women and treating them as dispensable. You took it better than I could. Months with the governors, you learn their ways.

'I'll see you at dinner, Riley. Polish your compliments for after the politics.'

Then you turned to me.

'Eight prompt. No excuses.'

Then we were alone, like so many times. The companionable silences. The ponies treading dandelions in the grass.

But overhead the dangerous sky, and the gun barrels out of sight in the bushes. Riley's world, where the dragon's mouth could open at any moment.

I poured him more whiskey.

'It's Friday,' he said, watching a grebe land on the lake. 'I have until Monday here. Two whole days to discuss your poem.'

I laughed.

'It doesn't matter,' I said. 'Not that much.'

But Riley was deadly serious. I knew then that I might have power under my fingers, glory eating out of my palm whenever I wrote.

'It matters,' he said. 'It matters to you, and it matters to me. But it also matters to those who matter, the people in Whitehall who want a box of reasons for what they're doing.'

'It's not that kind of poem.'

'But it might be. It might be very easily, from what I hear.'

There were stanzas everywhere. Some in letters, a few in people's minds. I'd been reading bits and pieces, talking about the structure. He had a good idea of the poem already.

So I went indoors and got the file. A blue square and the fleur de lys in the corners. My cursive scrawl.

I gave him a section, saw him blink a little.

'I'll read it aloud first,' I suggested.

Riley was very slow. Always was. He made you go

121

through the sense of every phrase, no allowance made for metaphor, or for symbolism.

'It's an allegory,' I would say.

'I know. But what does it mean. Tell me the way you would tell an old sailor, in Kinsale.'

'Be sensible, Riley. You're not an old sailor.'

But he was, in a sense. The shadows of the great battle were still there on the damaged retina, behind his patch. I felt I could lift the silk and see the armada moving.

Later he would tell the story in cocktail terms, a witty sequence of lantern slides to amuse a dinner table. But the guns blazing across the waves, the real tragedies, were still his secret.

So I simplified. I took my measures to pieces. Laid them out as prose. Then built them again, block by block, until he knew just as well what they meant as I did.

Then he argued closely. By now we had eaten. A pair of steaks with a bottle of claret, a dish of profiteroles. A breakfast of ham and eggs, and a pot of coffee. Another pot of coffee and some biscuits. A lunch of sandwiches in the yard, and a jug of Guinness.

Talk of love and war with the meals. Riley was always polite. He never brought his business to the board. Or his bawd, the rude said, to the business.

'Tell me, Riley,' you asked him once. 'Why won't you marry?'

But you knew the reason, as well as I did. He had been the Queen's man too long. We were both surprised when he gave you an answer.

'I may, Liz,' he said, stirring his coffee. 'I may now. Things have changed, you know. I have my own Liz.'

'Congratulations,' you said, really happy.

But he swung the conversation before we could ask any more. It was years before I learnt that his Liz was a name, and not a metaphor.

Out of his combat gear, in a blazer with a scarf and a

pair of flannels, Riley became more easy. He went for a walk with you in the wood, I remember, and then you were both back with an armful of bluebells.

He took to throwing sticks for Hengist, and was made the big dog's favourite when he never got bored. He would even sit, without moving, for hours, while he stroked him on his lap.

Sometimes he paused, and seemed to signal. But he never allowed the watchers in the bushes to come out and show their colours. He seemed to hate the security as much as we did.

On the telephone one night I thought he was giving orders to someone, in a voice tinged with anger. But he kept the call short, and insisted on paying.

Mostly, though, it came back to the poem. Hour after hour, we sat, indoors or out, arguing over the fine changes, the tunings and alterations he wanted.

It wasn't a matter of propaganda. He was far too subtle a reader for that. It was just that he felt, and he started to make me feel, that the underlying drive of the poem was being obscured by a kind of rhetoric.

'You must be clear,' he would argue. 'I don't mean plain, or banal. But it has to add up. Every link in the chain has to fit, and to hold. You have to cut, mostly. Then change a word here and a word there. A bare minimum, and it's done.'

But the minimum took time to argue. I wasn't always quick to fall in with his views, and he didn't sugar the pill. Not then.

But when the Rolls drew up, with the Irish flag flying on the bonnet, and when he was shaking hands, the row of medals glittering along his chest, he showed me what he thought.

'No-one, John,' he said. 'There's no-one else. I've spent two days with you on it, and I'm sure.' Then he added,

123

with a crooked smile, lightening his tone, 'I could do it myself perhaps, but I haven't the time.'

'You could lick me into a cocked hat,' I said. 'You and Hilary.'

'Not even Hilary,' he said seriously. 'It's a masterpiece.'

Then he was into the car, and there were motorbikes revving, and he was off to his airport, and his next meeting. The Minister of Defence, the Warden of the Stanneries, whatever he was then.

My friend Riley. The best poet in England, if only he'd bothered.

'The best critic, anyway,' you said, when I told you what he thought of the poem. 'I hope he marries, though. He needs a woman.'

But I wasn't sure. He still had his rainbow leader, with her butterfly wings. He had come by a coffin-ship and left by a hearse, and she still had her hands in his hair.

To Riley my poem was a poem, but it was also a tool to keep his grip on the cliff-face. The Queen had her needs.

20

We were in The Grand Hotel, stirring cream in abysmal coffee. Sean had his third lager, a late lunch.

'Paul quotes the bullocks,' he was saying, taking a thoughtful sip.

I heard the hammer go up in my head. You really do, with the pressure on.

'Now look,' I said, feeling your hand reach for my pulse.

But Sean had his finger up in the air, admonishing. There were times when Sean was a parody of a landlord, and this was one of them. Monocle and a blazer, I thought. You wear a blazer in May here, you have to be acting.

But his mannerisms amuse, they cool rage. I smiled, and I felt better.

'Tell me,' I said.

It was a warm day, larks rising. I hadn't wanted this meeting. We were on our way to hospital, a drive through bad country. So we'd stopped in the town square for a sandwich, and there was Sean, propping the bar, a country squire in his tweeds.

Tweeds or blazer. Take your pick. It was always one or the other. But he took his chances, Sean. You made a big mistake if you took him for a fool in fustian.

So in two minutes he had us over by the fire. Turf smouldering in the sun, an Irish paradox.

'Coffee,' he ordered, knowing your tastes at home. But

he never drank the stuff, was oblivious to its local awfulness.

There were men all round in shirt sleeves, perspiring Guinness, and here were we by the smoking grate, increasing our temperature with a brew of impossible granules.

I was jumpy to get away. But I listened.

'The point is this,' he was saying, 'They want a right of way. They say there was one before, of course.'

'That's insolence.'

I saw a man in braces rub his adam's apple with a raw forefinger, staring at me. He had a knife in his belt, a pistol under his arm-pit.

You see the antagonism, it takes on physical forms.

'Keep your voice down,' you said, stroking my knee, worried by my temper. But Sean had his own methods, temporizing by agreement.

'No, no, Liz,' he was saying. 'John's quite right. It is insolence, and it's meant as insolence. They want to annoy you. They want to make you do something silly, and then, of course, they've as good as won.'

I had my hand on my sword-hilt, I let it lie. Scoundrels and heretics.

'They say they have cattle to shift between their two farms. It means a long drive, round the edge of your land. Would save a lot of trouble, they say, if you let them cut across.'

'I'll see them in hell first.'

Sean laughed.

'You may at that,' he said, and then he was serious again. 'But they say they can't guarantee there won't be accidents, while your fences are weak.'

'They're not weak.'

'Well, they say they are. They say that's why the bullocks got into your yard, and frightened Liz.'

I watched the sparks lifting, the ash falling. This was

126

the way it was. They had me by the horns, neck on the block.

I hadn't told Sean about the bullocks, and now the Desmonds had stolen past me in my silence. They'd briefed him first.

'Sean, I'm sorry,' I said. 'I ought to have told you. What shall I do?'

'Let go, John,' he said. 'Ease up your horses. We'll hang them one day on the rope you give them now. You'll serve your interests best if you grant the right of way.'

But I wouldn't budge. Not then, anyway, in that bar of sweating aliens with their creamy beer and their meat-and-potato paunches. I wasn't ready, I felt too manipulated.

'I'll think about it,' I said.

Later, the cherry blossom fell like confetti around the moving car, and we nosed through lanes where the hedges had been barbered with spring fury.

'It's not working,' you said once, despairing.

I knew the symptoms, and I said nothing. I gathered all my energy into massive calm.

You had the tragic look you often see in me, a stare like a whippet, a silence clean as a razor. Then it came like blood from the bottle, a slow flood.

'I can't take it, the way you get. You let everything hurt you, everything make you angry. They're all against us, you think. They're after your money, your land, your things. It's paranoia.'

'No,' I said. 'It's true. You know it is. It's the way they are. The way everyone is, perhaps. But we have to accept the fact, and be reasonable. We have to try. That's why I came back.'

'It's not why. You came back for us, and with me. To get away from Linda. There was nowhere else. And it hasn't worked, it isn't working. She's here too. She's everywhere.'

I felt the blows go in, one after the other, under the lanterns of sycamore, the still-green pyramids on the chestnut leaves. The car moved in its own familiar silence, and the light sauntered on the bonnet.

I drew into a lay-by, killing the engine. There was bird-song suddenly, thrushes and robins under the trees, a melancholy jaundice of sunshine dropped in our laps. The speckled band, the snake of pain.

'I'm sorry, Liz,' I said. 'I shouldn't have been so upset. It's with not sleeping, I think.'

I put my hand on the huge bulge of our child. We'd been sleeping badly for weeks. The baby would move in the night when you were still. You would wake, and stir, and wake me, and I would be irritable.

Now we were both depressed, and calmer. I felt the rigid stretch of your skin, a carapace for a fisted soldier, a war-drum.

'Aquilina,' I said, stroking your navel like the tip of a helmet.

'Fred,' you whispered, happier now, mocking me.

We lay for a while enjoying the small ration of light, not speaking, more at ease. Then you were scratching your waist, ripping the skin in concentrated frustration, as if to speed the process of birth.

'Let's go,' you said, moodily. 'See what the doctor says.'

I started the engine, glided out from under the leaves. A tractor went by, too close, but the driver waved. I let him go, breathing steadily.

'Woof,' you said, pinching my cheek. 'Good boy.'

I laughed, and things were better again for a moment, for both of us. We were trying hard, and we kept on. But the day was against the English, or people in big cars, or simply Liz and John.

A bitch came out from a farm, snapping like a shark against my wheels, and I swerved and nearly scraped a wing, hearing you scream. I hated that, and I drove faster, and nearly hit a Micra on a bend.

But we got there, and intact. The awful hospital had its doors open, and we went in from stifling heat to a tomb chill.

There were sprigs of nuns everywhere, screens wide on a technicolour chapel. I nearly slipped on the greasy linoleum, catching your arm for support.

Along the glazed avenues of corridors, hung with posters of Lourdes, images of the Pope. Then down a flight of steely steps and into a reception area. Glove-tight rugs and a nurse like a boxer.

'This way, please.'

'I'm sorry we're late.'

'No problem.'

The doctor was there like Humpty-Dumpty, a broken egg with a yolk coming out. He had a bald skull and a bad scar, as if he'd just come home from a riot. There always seemed to be pus in the scar.

Dr Syntax.

That wasn't his name. It was how he appeared to approach the problem of there being a baby. We all do wrong, and we have to pay the price, a kind of VAT. The wages of sin attract a venereal amelioration tax.

He was pursing his lips.

'Five and a half pounds.'

I was reaching for my wallet, but he forestalled me.

'In weight, that is.'

He shook his head sadly.

'There would only be five in a hundred heavier, at this stage.'

'A chunky child,' you suggested, cheerfully.

'You could say that,' he agreed mournfully. 'You could say that. The heavier ones are sometimes the most trouble.'

'Same with sacks of coal,' I murmured, but I don't think he heard me.

So much for consolation. So much for putting the first time buyer in the right frame of mind for the transaction.

Then he had you on a rexine couch, his death's head with its stethoscope nodding at your mother's mound. A machine began to whirr.

Television. Behold, here is thy coming heir, the fruit of thy loins, lord of creation and decay. I squinted under my hands and saw the grainy, pulsing mouth, what passed for a child's heart grasping like an octopus.

I couldn't see the head, or a leg or arm, or any sign of sex. But she was there. He was there. They were both there, choosing which one to be.

'About the bill,' I said. 'When do I pay you for all this?'

He was writing notes on a dirty pad. He worked with a blunt pencil, objective correlative, so it seemed to me, for his mind.

'It depends,' he said, staring over a pair of tinted spectacles. 'An epidural could be expensive.'

'So we pay at the end?'

'So to speak,' he said. 'So to speak, yes.'

I don't know whether his gift for horror was natural or cultivated. He did it well, putting the frighteners on. He ought to have been in films.

'The old bugger knows his job,' you said, as we drove home. 'He knows the right answers to all the questions.'

'He treats you like shit,' I said flatly. 'I don't like it.'

'It's just his way. Doctors are all the same.'

'Perhaps.'

But I had a sense of cruel vengeance exacted whenever we opened our mouths, whenever they heard the voice of England from the womb.

Let them crawl and eat their own dung. There is no other way.

130

21

Sometimes I used to wake at night, thinking about it all. That May, I mean. Stick to that May. I put the limp and the pills aside, and the baby coming, and saw it through clear glass for a time.

I mean the situation. But not the beat of my heart, and the feel of going downhill to the tomb. The bog and the trees, I mean. The itinerants licking by in their cart. The invitations to balls and jousts.

This was a new Ireland. There was old blood and old money resting in easy chairs, the way they had always done. But there was fresh blood and fresh money, too. Flash cars and insane bungalows, and the same sly underdogs at the bottoms of all the barrels.

That was the trouble. They put the guards in green and the old embezzler into the Castle, and where was the difference. You rose a notch or two, you lashed the tinkers with your dry tongues, took your sticks through the bluebells. Anglo as the English.

I rose, once or twice. Walked over black boards on bare feet, feeling for spiders or dung-beetles in the hot weather. But there weren't any. Only the rough edges of what had always been there, the surfaces of discretion.

I used to take a seat on the cool stone of the south embrasure, staring out through the arrow-slit at the moon. You came and joined me once, and we sat like ghosts, white in our nakedness against the walls.

We talked for hours, but we got nowhere.

'You have to be Irish,' you told me. 'Even the kind of Irish I am. Then it makes what you might think sense.'

'But you're hardly Irish at all,' I objected. 'Your father was born in Wales.'

'I was born here.'

'So it comes to this. You give your life to their country, they lock you out. You have to have bog water in your veins before you can understand.'

'You're not locked out,' you said, sensing what I was thinking. 'You're welcome everywhere, so far as a foreigner can be.'

'But I'm not foreign. I've spent my life here.'

'Partly.'

The moon went up and into the clouds, a scimitar on a shield.

'They need some discipline,' I said savagely, 'the way we all do, the way we've always done.'

'Hug me,' you said. 'I need some discipline.'

So I took you back to the four-poster under the rafters, and there I solved the problem, as so many more have done.

But after the exquisite anguish, and the violent yielding, I still lay awake looking up through knot and worm towards the stars.

I was too involved. That was the trouble. You work for a cause, even a bad cause, you get used to the shapes of purpose. I had to exonerate the propaganda, the years of lying. I couldn't just come back and do nothing.

That's what they wanted, of course. The tiger in chains. The old administrator nailed down on his back with the little men climbing over his clothes.

Lie still and think of England. Forget the past and be a quiet exile. I thought of Tom in his grave, Riley in and out of his cell. I thought of O'Neill on the road, the Desmonds nibbling at my boundaries.

It wasn't so easy. I had to do something. You can't just

132

take the past and wrap it up in a parcel and drop it into the river. It comes back like vomit, into your throat, out of your mouth, over your shirt.

So I went to sleep with a resolution made. I would send my poem to Linda, let her help it into print if she could. It wasn't much, but it was something.

It drew a map of the sort of territory we had to live in. It defined the kind of man who might learn to survive there. It supported the Queen.

So the following morning, I rose first, and corrected a fair copy. I sent it through friends. Rolled up in a scroll, under a seal, with a covering letter. You share my paranoia, you never trust the posts.

But I told you what I was doing. You shrugged, and let me be. You knew, I suppose, I would send the poem. Poets are all the same, and you knew a few by now. We don't pass up a chance of publication.

You warned me. We were in the shrubbery, a mix of larch and spruce near the house, where the primroses were still alight. But under the green there were ants.

'It's a risk, John.'

'I know it is. But it's worth taking. I'm sure it is.'

Harland was laying gravel, from a wheelbarrow. He had the shot-gun slung over his back and a belt of shells around his waist. You can shoot crows, of course, but that wasn't what was in his mind.

I liked his caution, but you didn't.

'I hardly think you need the armoury, Harland,' you said, a bit rudely, perhaps.

But he was used to your criticism.

'Best to be sure, Liz,' he said. 'You never know'

'I agree,' I said, quickly. 'I do agree. Harland,' I added, riding over your anger, 'go over to Walton Hall, would you, and take this packet to Ralph St Lawrence. He knows it's coming.'

I handed over the scroll, those pressures of my brain,

and Harland weighed the poem in his oddly girlish hand. He takes care of his skin, it always looks whiter than it ought to be.

'With any luck,' I said, making conversation, 'that should be in London tomorrow. He's taking the ferry tonight.'

'With any luck,' said Harland, melancholy as ever. 'But the wind's high. They may sail late.'

He lingered, savouring the opportunity for some chat.

'It's the May Ball a week on Saturday,' he said suddenly.

'I know,' I said easily. 'We thought of going.'

Harland set the parcel down on the wheelbarrow. He wiped his lips with a wide striped handkerchief.

Then he breathed out sharply, and shook his head.

'It should be fine,' he said, uncertainly. 'But I'll come with you, just in case. I'll wait in the car.'

This was more than I'd bargained for. I felt a chill in the air, sensed that wind rising under the sun. There were glints of steel on the leaves wherever the light struck.

'That won't be necessary, Harland,' you said very carefully. 'But thank you for your concern. It was thoughtful of you. Now take the parcel over to the Hall, would you?'

'Of course. I just thought, with O'Neill being there, and the Desmonds, there might be trouble.'

Then he was gone. We stood in silence, hearing the crows building above our heads, the wrens rustling in the underbrush.

'O'Neill,' I said, furiously. 'Surely they wouldn't invite O'Neill?'

'We pay now,' you said. 'We all pay, it's the same for master and man.'

You were bitter enough. But I could see you were shaken, too. You didn't want to rub shoulders with people who'd tried to kill you.

134

I picked up a handful of gravel, felt it run through my fingers. Dirty stuff, dear at the price it had been.

'Perhaps he's right,' I said. 'A gun in the car could come in useful.'

But you weren't over your built-up annoyance at Harland's need to turn your precious garden into a military camp.

'I'm not going,' you said flatly, picking up a fallen rake and attacking the path. 'You can take Harland and go by yourself.'

It took an hour of sweetness, and a pot of my best coffee, borne steaming out on a silver tray, to stay your fury. But at last we sat on the terrace, a view before us towards the hills, and the crenellations like iron waves on the heat haze, and the world seemed safe again.

'There'll be hundreds there,' I said. 'I doubt if we'll even see the Desmonds. As for O'Neill, I think that's Harland guessing.'

But I wasn't sure. A man in a cart came by as we sat, a lanky donkey hauling a load of wood to a halt. I went down the stone spiral and out the door, and he dropped to the ground, reaching his cap off. It might have been forty years ago.

'O'Connor,' he said. 'Saving your presence. James O'Connor.'

I held out my hand and I thought for a moment he might be going to kneel and kiss an invisible ring.

'Spencer,' I said. 'I'm John Spencer. How are you?'

'Aye, John. I know who you are.'

Then he came to the point very fast for an Irishman. Of course, perhaps he wasn't Irish. I never knew.

'I hear you're worried about the state of the road.'

'Well, it is bad.'

'You're wanting those who share the use of the road to share the cost of some gravel. Is that it?'

'It is.'

'I'm willing. O'Connor's willing. Remember that.'

Then he was back on his cart, lifting the reins, and the tottering donkey was on its way with what, I then suddenly realized, was probably a load of my wood.

I went indoors, laughing, and told you. Meanwhile Hengist lay in the yard, snoring his lunch off, and this was another warm day when he didn't bother to announce or accost a stranger.

May was the lull before the storm, though. Things were going to change.

I felt a strange pricking in my joints, and my leg was worse than usual. It seemed an omen.

22

In a stone room the chill comes off, even in summer. I had a bench by the window, the small oriel. Was writing. Polishing rather, the way you polish dull silver.

> No gaudy roll-calls of who's who
> Or scrolls of names in peacock dyes
> Or cobwebby mythologies.
> Only the plain knight and the Cross
> And Una with her maddening eyes.

You write it once, you write it a dozen times. Balancing the epithets, extracting the crud. The ink flying out of the nib across the cheap pads, the vellum. Whichever.

It was late, long after four in the morning. I had my feet in fur boots, a gown around my shoulders. The single candle flame like a sentry, straight up in the sconce.

You can see by one. Even flickering by one, but there wasn't a wind. That May, there was no wind. Some nights I sat out after twelve with the flames going up like pillars out of the candelabra. No more sideways movement than in a crack regiment.

It helps, late at night. There's nothing to interrupt, and the words flow.

> As in a mine
> The shaft sinks lower and the lights
> Show donkeys as the cables whine
> And veins of minerals and flights
> Of heady steps.

I went to and fro, like an old man with a lantern. A caretaker, opening doors, visiting neglected galleries. Every time I took up the poem, it became a strange house, a little different from the way I'd left it before.

I had so much to do. Mending a fuse in the basement, freeing a stuck shutter in an attic. Loosening the rhythm in Canto Four, I would find a dud rhyme, like a spent bulb, and have to go back in my mind to look for a replacement.

Sometimes it seemed hardly a metaphor. The poem and all its furnishings was as real to me as my own castle. It took on a ghostly resonance, and I lived with it, and through its rooms.

> The close
> Green-woven ivy round the door
> Admits you to a world verbose
> With cunning, where the sly adore
> Your least appeal, and where there's more
> To keeping calm than walking through.

I began to let the verses reflect my own state of mind, and the allegory flowered. It became infected, infecting, and I found a game of royal tennis in progress between my lines and our hostess at the Hunt Ball I had just left.

> She could split a pear
> At fifty paces in a fight
> With one slim arrow, set alight
> And flaming in the camel's eye,
> The cool of noon, where no-one fell
> Save Barajasus, in the stye.
> She was an amazon, of warrior's dye.

The Ball had had few surprises. Lady Jane, with her eyes like hunting crops and her breasts like fox's teeth, had received us under the *porte-cochère*, where the car had drawn in from the rain.

138

Sir Brian had already been on the floor, adept with someone's daughter in a jaunting reel, and his nimble escort had been left to do the honours alone. She was good at this, a rakish wasp in a gold stole.

I kissed her cheek, and soon had her old, eager lips at my mouth.

'Liz,' she added, though, talons out for a squeeze at your undefended arm, and we all seemed friendly enough while the spears of hail lashed at her gravel.

Harland had been persuaded to stay at home, but I'd compromised with his caution, a little unwisely I now thought on the brink of peaceful hilarity, by carrying the loaded shot-gun on the back seat. Mercifully, I had it out of sight in a croquet box.

'Running guns, John,' a voice boomed at my elbow, as we dawdled under the coffering. But fortunately it was only Jack Russell, a yapping drunk like his canine name-sake, too small to be seen.

'Bananas for cocktails,' I said smoothly. 'I'll see that you get some, Jack.'

Then we were in. A blunt retainer with a lot of rings was parking the car for me, and I could live with Jack laughing. After all, a cousin of his, in dress uniform, had fallen with a bullet in his guts on those very steps, and that wasn't more than forty years ago.

Some of them soon forget. There's a case for weapons, even when the masters go dancing. Perhaps particularly when the masters go dancing.

'Forty years is a long time,' you said, when I put this idea to you.

'Living memory.'

'Besides, there's doubt about who shot the man. I've heard Jack himself say it might have been an outraged husband.'

'Or an angry tenant. I've heard the stories. But they

don't alter my point. It's always dangerous to be seen as English here.'

The Ball was well attended. A slew of gentry, plenty of merchants, and, of course, the hunting set, which means what you will, these days. You couldn't tell from the men in their penguin suits.

But the women gave it away. Costume jewellery and thick figures. Too much cream coffee down behind that surging cleavage.

I get snobbish, I suppose. The day was they wouldn't have been let in to hand the claret. We had girls from the shires then, with haunches like hunters. All English roses.

There was a good bar, and I propped it with one old crony after another, while the young went by to their revels. A stooping soldier I didn't know had several rum and cokes with me, while we admired the chandelier.

He voiced my own paranoia, and I liked him for it.

'I always feel safer when I step ashore off that boat at Fishguard,' he said. 'You see the Union Jack, and it's like a security symbol.'

There was muscle everywhere. I noticed it while he was talking. The boys with badly fitting jackets and wandering eyes. Bulges under their arm-pits.

They were being careful, after all. More than I'd thought, at first. Relax then, put your fear back in its scabbard.

I turned to order another round of drinks, and then I saw Hugh O'Neill, and my stomach dropped and went through the floor. I don't suppose my hand was shaking, but I felt it was.

He had something very flash on, ivory sharkskin with a crimson sash. His hair was back like a thirties bandleader's, and he moved as if he was in a club he owned. I could swear he snapped his fingers and someone brought him a whiskey.

'Grander than last time,' he said, nodding at the soldier,

140

who went down in my estimation by seeming to know him. 'You well, John? You look well.'

'Excuse me,' the soldier said, and went up a notch again in my rating.

O'Neill watched him go, smiling at a circle of friends who seemed to have materialized around him, a sort of protective, supporting halo.

'I remember the Colonel's wife last year,' he said. 'She was so pissed she couldn't swing on the chandelier. Fell off and wet her knickers in the punch-bowl. Surprised us all. Her chimpanzee performance was usually the climax of the Ball.'

There was a ripple of derisive laughter around the ring, a sycophantic echo.

'Mind you, I know what he means about the Union Jack. After all, I used to salute the bloody thing every day myself. It's hard to shake the habit.'

I felt enraged and awkward, in equal proportions.

'You here as a paying guest, Hugh?' I said.

It was the best I could do, a childish gibe.

'Aren't we all?'

But I didn't like the situation. They had me at the centre of their mob, a badger being baited by hounds.

'I danced with Liz,' O'Neill was saying, and it took a moment to sink in. 'She moves well with the baby. A pity about your leg.'

Then he was gone, leaving me trembling. One of them stubbed a cigarette out in my empty glass, a cousin of the Desmonds. I knew his face.

I propped my cane in the crook of the wall, and picked up a lonely girl with a dress half-way down her thighs, and a blank look, stoned as a clown, and I leaned on her three times around the pinched floor, and past the band, grinning lecher with his face in a wench's neck.

Then I saw you, alone by the wall, and I broke the clinch and said, excuse me, and reeled over to you, and

141

saw you smiling, pleased to see me approaching. The world was all right again, and we were together.

'You danced with him,' I said accusingly. 'With O'Neill.'

But you were in a good mood. You laughed.

'Of course I didn't,' you said, hugging me. 'I haven't danced with anyone. He was winding you up.'

We stayed side by side after that, except when I let you dance with Sir Brian, the fornicating tornado, as his partners often dubbed him. But I knew your belly would hold him off.

'Try Mary-Anne,' I suggested to him, as we rested near to the buffet. 'I thought she was ripe for it after the last lambada.'

So we watched him sail like a small sexual tank towards the lonely girl I had danced with.

'Was she?' you asked me, doubtfully.

'Hardly,' I said, soberly. 'It froze my cock off.'

You hit me with your hand-bag, and we wrestled like a dozen other excited couples, as the tempo of the Ball grew hotter. There were trips upstairs into squealing bedrooms for several, and we lay on the landing in the darkness, hand in hand, and thigh to thigh, listening to a gypsy singing and a baronet playing the tin whistle.

It was a good Ball, as I say. Lady Jane was said to have screwed an Italian in a batman outfit, and the nine virgins, three well-known trios of teenage daughters, were initiated into the mysteries of the French kiss. There were fights over handsome waiters, and bets about stallions.

All in all, an excellent ball. Ending up with a lot of vomit in a few buckets, and a little spermatozoa in a lot of condoms.

So I drove back, aware even as I left of the watchful, undrinking muscle in the hall and the shrubberies, and I put you to bed with your clothes on, and I went through

142

a maze of corridors to the stone room where I keep the poem, and I turned to my polishing.

> The ground
> Is closing, and the hellish hound,
> Cerberus, who guards Pluto's gates
> Has let him go.

It was a good night for the poem, and I closed the book near to six, when the light was back in the room, and I went through to where you were sleeping, and I lifted your ice-pink skirt, and I made love to you, willing and delighted, until you were wide awake, and came in my arms.

The baby lay between us, and kicked, and then we fell asleep, and the sun warmed the sheets, and the baby was only a remote presence, a steady drumming like the orangemen commemorating the Battle of the Boyne.

But it would be here, and soon.

23

You look at the map now, it's one island. All coloured green. Like the leprechauns, like the emeralds they say the Vikings threw in the bogs.

I had the atlas out in the library, in the sun. It was four parts in my time. A ring of forts round the Pale, then the south and the west and the north. Then it was only two, the north we could hold and the rest.

I used to ride in the Landrover, with the border patrols. In and out of Monaghan, looking for your man. But we never found him. Not the one essential man, whose death would bring the rebellion to an end, unite the island in our own image.

There were too many of him, or else he never existed. Or both. He might have been O'Neill once. He might still be O'Neill, if gangsterism was the way through.

No one could squeeze two sorts of dough together to make one country. Two sorts of steel. The sharp steel of the north and the flexible steel of the south. It would never make one sword.

Except in the dreams of men like O'Neill, who still wanted a forged blade, like a flight of bombers. Who couldn't bear a loose friendly association, where everyone muddled along. Being polite, and getting nowhere.

I understood O'Neill, and his dream. It was Riley's dream, only upside down. My own dream, I suppose. Even now, on my rubbered cane, my own dream.

I looked out across the sheep and the bleating calves, and it hit me. That's why I remember the moment so well,

144

when Harland came in with the mail. May 13th, an evil day.

I had the map on my desk, and the need for some kind of real union in my mind. A union of ideas. A union fed out of my poem.

'Put them there, Harland,' I said idly, seeing the beak of his face in the doorway, the falcon stooping.

But I didn't reach at once for the thin sheaf of letters. I let them rest where he set them, under the brass lion of St Mark, beyond my ink-wells.

I got up and went over to the window, setting the globe spinning. The fluting cherubs went round and round. The whales blew, and the curlicues on the names ran over the tails of mermaids, and the monsters.

I thought about Francis, rolling his bowls before the battle. I thought about Philip, in that earlier war, when we had to redefine Dutch courage. I thought about Riley, carrying the flag to the edge of the world.

Then I went back and started opening the envelopes, facing the accusing stare of the Black Prince in my waste-paper basket, a sleeping lady disturbed by snow as I shredded what I didn't want, on her fur.

Time stopped, though. It does sometimes. I felt winded then, when I came back, realizing there had been a shock, like a heart attack, and I was down on my chair, absorbing it.

The lawyer's name, on the headed paper, a sort of relief, a snail beading. Then the pompous opening, the dear sir. The phrase, I am acting for Linda, and then her stage name. The unreality of my Linda, my once Linda, appearing in her make-up, at this time of day, as an actress.

But she wasn't acting, or at any rate the lawyers weren't. I read the letter once, then I read it again. Then I went over to the hatch, and poured a quarter tumbler of Jameson's, it was all there was.

145

Then I thought better of taking it neat, and went through to the sink, and added some water, and then, I felt I had to do something to keep my hands from trembling, some ice.

I took it all back in the library, and sat down again, and now I had to go through the letter again, a third time. I had to be sure. Then I drank, slowly, rewarding myself. You've done well, have a drink, you know what it means. They mean to destroy you.

'That's what it comes to,' I told you, when I called you in. 'She wants my blood. Shaken, but not stirred, and my liver chopped in slices for a topping.'

By then, you had read the letter, too, and the sun was bright as brass on the two chairs we faced each other in. You were beautiful, I had time to see that, a little girl in blue, hiding a plum pudding under her dress.

You might have been furious, but you weren't. You might at least have allowed yourself an 'I told you so.' But you didn't.

You simply let your face cloud, and your brain move fast, and then you came over and sat in my lap, and hugged me. We stayed for a long time like that, without saying anything, and I felt the need to start trembling and go on trembling until I shook like a jelly all over gradually recede, and become a thing I could manage.

'Thank you, Liz,' I said at last, near to tears. 'You were right, and I was wrong. I'm sorry.'

But you frowned, shaking your head. Then you got up, and walked to the window, thinking. A swallow went past, and it was spring, but neither of us was aware of peace, or growth.

'She's gone mad,' you said, decisively. 'She's gone completely off her rocker.'

The Black Prince leapt out of the basket, arching her back. She sniffed at the lawyer's letter, now on the floor, scratched it with her paws. She seemed to agree with you, and she knew Linda well.

'She promised to help me,' I said, unbelieving. 'I just don't understand. She never took any interest in my poems before.'

But you weren't anxious to see reason in what you saw as violence.

'She wants to keep you,' she said. 'Any way she can. If it's not love, she'll settle for hate. She's out of her mind.'

I had a paper-knife in my hand, a wooden pokerwork affair, and I realized I was jabbing it viciously, in and out of my blotter. I laid the thing down, interlacing my hands, beginning to shake again.

'I need to talk to Riley,' I said, musing aloud. 'He'll advise me what I should do.'

You were beside me again, holding the glass to my lips, calm and serious.

'Drink it up,' you said. 'Then I'll get you another, and a cup of tea, and a biscuit.'

I drank, fast, and the whiskey scorched me, and I realized that you'd switched a neat one for the watered down one I'd poured for myself. I coughed, swallowing, grateful and outraged at the same time.

Then I felt better suddenly, warm and invulnerable. It's better than drugs, always is. You can keep your morphine, your crack and your ecstasy. Drown them in drink, your sorrows, that's the way.

'Thanks, Liz,' I said. 'I'm sorry to be so shaky.'

But you brushed aside my apologies, running through the letter again, with the Black Prince round your ankles.

'Most of this is bluff,' you said. 'It's lawyer's jargon. They're trying to put the frighteners on.'

'I know,' I said. 'I can see it is. But we both know what the Official Secrets Act means. Even a breath of suspicion, and they'll put my poem on ice for years. It's just the cover for what she really wants. But it's a strong suit.'

147

A tractor went by, Harland dour at the wheel. He was on his way for cigarettes, to the inn. I waved, easily, but, of course, he didn't see me. I was feeling it very necessary to seem normal.

You were shaking your head, not agreeing with me.

'It's very unlikely,' you said. 'After all, you've been out of Intelligence for ten years. You couldn't know anything recent to give away. Besides, they're trying to clean up their act. They wouldn't want to be seen as vindictive.'

'I could make some changes,' I said. 'Riley will know what to do.'

The Black Prince was on my lap now, a licorice whirl of affection. I stroked her back, watching the portrait of Sir Walter Scott on the wall. He was reading an essay to a club in Edinburgh. He looked young and bored.

'It isn't her business, anyway,' you said. 'She'd be seen as biased, in view of her motivation. Which is, to protect her own interests.'

'The libellous portrait of my client,' I agreed, quoting the lawyer's letter.

Then I sat back, and thought about it. What Linda claimed had a germ of truth. I'd drawn on her, and our married lives, it was true, several times in the poem. It's what you do, it's what we all do, a writer would naturally have known that.

After all, she did the same herself. Picking a trait here and a characteristic there, and weaving them into a stage portrayal, a film cameo. It's the stuff of drama.

But what she did, and what I'd done in my poem, was hardly libellous. The very reverse. I'd violated some rights of privacy, perhaps, but in the process I'd made her seem even more glamorous. A mythic figure. A goddess of power.

'As for Sylvanus,' you said, reading on. 'What she says

148

is absurd. She must have gone round the bend in a Maserati. A hundred miles an hour.'

It was true. With malevolence, it appeared, I'd intruded upon the private life of my son, when I'd made him a wood nymph, and a page at court. Readily recognizable by his golden curls, and his place of birth.

'It's bollocks,' you said. 'You have to get on the blower to Riley now.'

But that wasn't so easy. I drew blank, as I'd feared I might, at all his old haunts. He might be in prison, he might be out on bail. He wasn't at home.

'She's cunning,' you said, later that night, as we ate our supper, a solitary pair at the end of a polished oval. Using the full resources of the house, that's what we called it, the nights we fed alone in the dining-room. But it gave us a sense of elegance, and it aired the silver.

I sliced my gammon, and I took a mouthful of pineapple. Thinking hard always makes me hungry.

'I could try Sean,' I said warily. 'But, after all, it's another country now. He might not be much help.'

'You could go to London. Try your solicitor there.'

'Yes,' I said. 'But I'm not sure that I want to. Not with the baby coming.'

You smiled, and squeezed my wrist, and I looked up and admired the arcs of the fleur-de-lys in the ceiling. I thought, irrelevantly, of how much Linda would have liked the arches over the doors, and the vaulting.

'I hate her guts,' I said, laying down my knife and fork. 'I really do. I'll never forgive her for this.'

But you were gloomy, though pleased.

'It's what she wants,' you said, sadly. 'We never forget our enemies.'

Then I took my sundae, and enjoyed my strawberries and ice cream. The past had died for me, and I was hungry for the future.

'I wrote in praise of the Queen,' I said, reaching for coffee. 'It's wicked to accuse me of treason.'

'But she is wicked,' you said. 'You have to accept that.'

It was hard, though. I remembered too many kindnesses in another country, another epoch.

24

They came in from four sides. Quiet men, with good suits and white cuffs. Nothing conspicuous, nothing you might have thought was threatening.

But they checked the curtains. Ran their hands under the table-cloth and the lamp-shades. Were very careful about the lines of vision.

'Clear,' one of them said, in what I assume was a miniature transmitter. But it fitted into the hollow of his hand, like a coin.

He didn't smile, catching my eye. None of them did. They behaved like the night soil men we used to have as a child in Cheapside, as if they weren't there, as if you couldn't see them.

But there was a difference. There was no sense of being ashamed of their job. Not about these men. They walked like princes, which perhaps they were.

Riley and I were in the lounge, with double whiskies. A florid, airy place, with a lot of chintz and cushions.

I'd been warned of how it would be. The kind of high security that you feel like a leather skin. A mixture of smooth and tight.

'We'll arrive first,' Riley had told me, in the black Volvo that met us at the air-field. 'There may be as many as eight others, I don't know. Including herself, of course.'

The summons had come by surprise, and I wasn't ready for it. Sheenane breaking into my concentration, like smashing a precious cup. She was good at that.

'There's a man at the door. Sir. With a telegram. He says he has to give it to yourself in person.'

Those dull, hammer eyes going into my brain, as I sat by the window trying to write. Watching the trails of bird muck on a pane too high to clean.

'I'll come, Sheenane,' I said, shoving Hengist aside.

He was always hot on her heels now, quick to appreciate the opportunities of intrusion. I shouldered him off the remains of my lunch, a chicken bone and a shred of curling ham.

'Give him the meat,' I said, over my shoulder, repenting, as I went for the stairs. 'But make sure he eats it out in the corridor.'

It would offer her something to do, other than rubbing holes in veneer with white spirit, or tipping fresh trifle into rubbish bags. I went downstairs, feeling efficient.

It wasn't the usual boy with a bicycle. This was a man, as Sheenane had said, and he'd come in a car. A rather splendid car, with flags on the bonnet.

There were two men, to be precise. The driver, in peaked cap and boots, who was holding the back door open. And the rather elegant androgyne who minced out of the rear seat with a crocodile brief-case chained to his wrist.

He said nothing, while the driver took a key from his pocket and did the ritual unlocking.

'You do yourselves well at the Embassy nowadays,' I suggested, nodding at the carriage and horses.

Well, it might have been. I'd seen these royal messengers before. A luxurious breed, in my opinion.

'Masters retired, has he?' I asked.

I wasn't going to behave like a ninny to please their perverse notion of the proprieties. I'd seen these crocodile boxes unlatched before, and very unimportant mice had come sniffling out.

'Thir John ith in Mothambique,' the androgyne lisped. 'I'm deputithing for him.'

He didn't offer a name, only the sealed envelope without a stamp. I broke the seal, and started to read. I didn't want to, but I knew they wouldn't go away without a reply. A signature before witnesses. That was the drill.

So I took my time, irritating them as much as I could. I didn't like young Monkdowne-Pisscocke, or whoever he was.

There were two envelopes in the envelope. The invitation, in embossed gold. An unbelievable, rainbow affair. And Riley's terse covering note.

'We'll pick you up at five. On Thursday. Just you, no Liz, I'm afraid. You'll be gone two days.'

There was a light wind, and the messenger's curly hair was blowing like an angel's wig. I felt an insane desire to chuck his cheeks.

'Hand me the receipt book,' I said, and I deliberately riffled through it before signing. 'I should get yourself a name,' I added, reaching the book back to the driver, a careful insult. 'It would help communication.'

Then I turned on my heel. But they were already moving. They didn't want to waste time standing still in shooting range of so many trees.

There might be friendly relations, at government level. But you wouldn't take too many risks, not in the boondocks.

Come to that, I didn't blame them. The Union Jack was a potent symbol, fluttering on the radiator cap.

Riley met me outside Dublin. Some military strip, I never knew its name. They'd sent a van to the house, and I'd ridden, not very comfortably, in the back.

The private jet was better. A few swivel chairs in a saloon with a cocktail cabinet and a video machine. The sort of thing a millionaire does deals in.

We watched a film that wouldn't have been given a

153

certificate in the new republic, while the bodyguards licked their lips and sucked mints.

'Beware of strange women,' you'd said, seeing me off with an apple and a sandwich. But you hadn't imagined the dangers would be celluloid.

I stared at the pumping buttocks and missed you. I don't think the bodyguards missed anyone, crossing and uncrossing their legs in the heat. Riley was asleep, lost in his own dreams.

I envied his innocence, if that's what it was. I could never sleep, on the verge of something important. Always too highly strung, too busy balancing alternatives.

'You'll be on her left,' Riley told me, as the white hawthorn and the flowering chestnuts went by.

Twisting roads, Norfolk at it most guileful.

'She'll run the conversation her own way. About this and that, you never know. Racing, condoms. But she'll come to the poem.'

'In her own time.'

'In her own time, John. She can't be hurried.'

The car swerved to the right, accelerated, then made a sharp – a very sharp – left-angling turn. I was thrown over against Riley, then took a grip on the tassel hanging by my ear.

'Does she like the poem? What are the signs?'

Riley laughed, though silently.

'Don't be silly, John,' he said. 'We're dealing with naked power. It moves in its own grooves. You'll make an impression. You'll have a chance. That's all we can say.'

So there it was. She and I together for an hour and a half at a lunch table. Nothing more, nothing less.

I took another double whiskey, and a few nuts to go with this one. There was a curious smell in the room, a sort of heavy perfume. I don't know what it was.

'A debilitating nerve gas,' Riley said, when I asked him,

154

but I wasn't in the mood to find it as funny as he evidently did.

We were all waiting, the manager, the waiters, the invisible bodyguards. There was a clock ticking, a Georgian thing in a glass dome. A lot of time seemed to flow away under its clappers before anything happened.

Then they came, in two waves. The first wave was a slew of Lords and a General. Even, I think, a professor somebody, but the sort of professor expecting a knighthood.

I shook hands, did my smile. They all looked less nervous than I felt, but this didn't help. They took large drinks, and began to chatter.

When her own party came, I scarcely noticed. There had been a pair of Range Rovers, unobtrusive grey, parking in the forecourt. Then everyone in the room was on their feet, even me, and the introductions were moving.

Trumpets, perhaps. I don't know. A rattle on a side drum, or simply a blast of thunder. Then she was there, unsmiling.

A wasp woman in a golden dress, encrusted with pearls. Bouffant hair, immaculately lacquered. And the dragons racing up her sleeves.

Surprisingly young, surprisingly small. Her ankle bandaged up to the knee, she must have fallen. A headdress of blue feathers. Her hands.

Moving, always moving. Her body running on wheels. To and fro. A word here, a word there. That full command of the script, and the courtiers genuflecting, preening like peafowl.

Then we were seated. Then we were eating. I don't remember eating, though. Only talking. My tongue seemed to be on the end of her leash, and it yapped yapped happily along while she took it out for a walk.

I was mesmerized.

'We go this way,' she said, moving her hands to the

155

left. 'And then we go that,' and her hands moved to the right. 'I was taught the rules as a child.'

So her conversation started with me, on her left, and at half past two, she swung it, with perfect ease, and engrossed the lord on her right, a pompous fox with a limp rose in his buttonhole, in a dialogue about life in Saskatchewan. About selling chips in Bradford. Who knows? She kept her voice down.

I was stuck with a dark virago, pressing my knee under the table. Her breath all garlic and almonds. But her conversation presumed that I was the Duke of Bomberg. That's how it sounded, and I basked idly in the vile imposture.

'Let's motor on,' I heard the lady say.

But I was the talk of yesterday, at least for the moment. I had to make do with my castle in Bucks, and my sly wife who had vanquished my neighbour at loo. Or in the loo, I was never quite sure.

So I coasted along, and thought back. What exactly had she been saying? Not a word about my poem, unless in symbol. But that was possible, of course.

'Auden, yes. A real old dear. He took me for walks, you know. But I never read his verse. Do you?'

So we went over Auden. Auden, or Wyatt. His alexandrines, or were they? His false quantities. But they have a rhythm, don't they?

She ate nothing. I remember that. Her fork separated the awful fish, the immaculate steak. Left it in pieces. Hovered over the pudding, prodding, neglecting.

A colostomy had been rumoured. How old was she? Nobody knew. Too old to eat? It looked like it. She must have a drink or two and some pills, in private, before she came.

'So you used to teach poetry. Could you teach it to me? Do you think? I was never any good at school.'

156

With my tutors, whatever it was. I went over it all, as a hand squeezed my thigh, and her breathing gassed me.

'I am not the Duke of Bomberg,' I gasped. 'I am John Spencer, a poet. A plain mister, madam.'

My thigh was released, and the witch was silenced. I thought back over what the lady had said. Her house in the north, her childhood home. The low trees there, scorched by the wind. Stags on the moor, and falcons in the hills.

I remember her lifting her glass once, to Riley at the other end of the table. And him lifting his, in return. A secret signal.

Then we were on our feet, moving round. A circulation of coffee, petit fours.

'Harry, dear. Shall we tootle over to Viney's?'

They were going, four or five of them. But on the way to the door, she passed me, leading me with her for a few yards.

'I like your new verses, Mr Spencer. Why don't you publish them? I think you ought to.'

But she spoke very quietly, and between two rooms, and I doubt if anyone heard except myself, and I'm sure there was nothing recorded on the tape they always had going in the lunch room.

So it was good news. But it wasn't something definitive. She hadn't openly praised the poem in front of the others.

I felt dizzy with excitement, and then a sense of depression, and this lasted all the way back in the Volvo, and then in the aeroplane, and then in the van.

But you were pleased, when I got home.

'It's good news,' you said. 'It will stop Linda, for sure.'

I hoped so, but I wasn't convinced. I felt a lot still depended on Riley, and Riley had had no time to speak to me before I left. He'd been lured into some military cabal, and I'd last seen him with his head over a map and a brandy, as the car arrived to take me to the airfield.

The driver gave me a note, as I boarded the plane.

'A start, anyway,' it said, in Riley's hand.

A start. Well, it was something. But I was feeling tired.

25

One day there won't even be a lake any more. It won't even be water. There may be sheep, like rocks, in the bowl, poking their heads up in the gaps between the stringy reeds in a marsh.

You go out in a boat alongside the kingcups, and the ducks rise like a flight of arrows. Clean from fluid to air. You look back and you see the house like a natural cliff, something you might defend for ever. A bastion.

But it won't last. It'll all change.

You go down through the pickpockets in a wave of stink like a midden. But you feel the hilt of your sword and you know you're safe. So far as it goes.

It took me a long time to see that it had to be prose. I came home with half of the poem locked in a steel box, in a spring binder. I thought it would do.

I went over it every day, revising and changing. I still do, in my bad moods. I even say I may print a few sequences in the back.

Lay it out the way it was going to be. All in rhyme and metre, floating nines, you know. That was the idea.

But we can't all be Shakespeare. We can't all be Webster, even. Mummers and mouthers. Holding the stage against a gaggle of groundlings.

Far as the closet goes, it's prose nowadays. You won't find many folk who'll turn the leaves of a book of verse. Women, maybe. Women, and a few students, for a few years. Before they get their guitars going.

You write a song, or you turn a monologue, you're right as rain. Might be in the money, even.

But otherwise, it's prose. You can polish the sentences, you can put in some cadences and a bit of rhetoric. But it mustn't rhyme, and it can't have too many images, and it shouldn't need to be read aloud.

It has to read easy, and then they'll listen. Slides down like a page of a popular newspaper, and there they are. Eating out of your hand.

I don't know how much of this will do the job, really. After I'm gone, you can go through the pages, Liz, and cut the crap.

More the story than what you say, of course. A narrative with a notion. Machiavelli with a bit of music. That's the ticket.

> Set round with gibbets, dire Despair,
> Who never dug a shallow grave,
> Sat rocking by the dead one, bare
> And bleeding, with the blade still there.

That's how it feels. Does on some days, anyway, sweating here at the white table above the traffic, waiting for you to come home from the chemist's.

Give or take a week, there's not much left. There can't be. You don't last long, when your bones all freeze together, the way mine do.

That's what I told Gaby. Met him today at Lavery's. The last bar in Cheapside with sawdust on the floor.

They ought to write it up in a brochure and get the Americans in. Quadruple the price of the drinks.

'Preserve us,' Gaby said.

He still has the squint and the muffler. Must have seven hundred thousand stashed away in bonds, and he dresses like a bum. An Edwardian bum.

Writing it down. Talking easy. As if you were here, Liz.

Like you soon will be. Like you soon won't be, when the bones lock. It helps. It keeps me calm.

I bought him a whiskey and soda. Nobody else would ask for the stuff any more, but they keep a bottle for Gaby. I had my long Harry, with a twist of lemon, and we sat under the Punch titles, in an alcove.

'Long time,' Gaby said, spreading his hands. 'Even the letters appear to have.'

A gesture, as if launching a small paper boat, on a pond. His. A grimace, mine. And a pair of young homosexuals going by, one saying to the other, with a nudge and a nod at Gaby. Didn't he used to be in films?

Gaby smiled, hearing that. The vanity has not deserted its oracle. He brushed an imaginary crumb from his gaiters. Yes, he has gaiters now. A leather pair, with rotting laces, like a diseased bishop's.

'I come from the leper colony of Lambeth, and I meet the Cato of Abbeyknockmoy.'

'Doneraile, actually,' I corrected him.

But Gaby was already unrolling one of his prepared monologues. You remember the sort of thing. It hasn't altered. The words coming out like a Japanese scroll being gently pulled from a beautiful lacquer case.

'Deliciously apt, indeed, our encounter. The glance of discerning, alienated minds in a coign of derelict Albion. Poor capital, thy swags are down, thy airy festoons droop with a weight of grief.'

'Another whiskey, Gaby,' I suggested, by way of diversion, but he wasn't quite ready to be put from his course. He did actually have something to say.

'As yours, laird of Cork,' he resumed, as I fell back on my stool. 'They tell me Our Lady of Former Favours can still trouble the waters with her poison wand. That is, divert the even current of your now admittedly much-disinfected allegory. I mean, ban your prose.'

I woke at that, slammed my long glass down on the

161

hideous table. A girl in black lashes with bare, rouged nipples put her tongue out at me for a noisy, ill-mannered lout.

'I didn't know they could,' I said.

'A change in the law, my darling. A little shift of the pincers with which our lords and masters grip us.'

Always was a good lawyer. Still is, despite the fancy brocade he likes to talk.

'They can do more or less what they choose,' Gaby admitted, studying his awful fingernails. 'She may win, she may lose. But she has plenty of new statutes to prop her bids on.'

'The lady,' I began.

'Is a modulating quantity, John. But, yes. I will drink another whiskey with you. That we may turn our minds to less poignant matters.'

I got him the whiskey, propelling myself through nudging rubber and abrading leather.

But I didn't wait to hear what he wanted to say. I left my second long Harry half drunk on the table, and I shoved the revolving door like a carousel, and I went through into the grinding rain, and the dust.

My leg was good for some reason, rage maybe, and I kept a good pace up the road through the mackintoshes and the umbrellas. Two rival clans, Italian curves and Scottish swashbuckle.

I had that heightened, fanciful feeling I sometimes get from mid-day liquor. The water streamed on my spectacles, and I drank in London filth in solution. Coughed once or twice, and began to hate that road.

Outside the Law Courts, all street and stone, I gave in to the weather. Saw the light of a cab, and lifted my cane. Say this for it, the crippled warrior method usually works.

He actually had the door open.

'Lousy day, mate.'

'You're telling me.'

162

But he wasn't. I wasn't letting him. I had the slider of glass to, and I sat back in the corner, staring away at the falling rain, and suddenly rather enjoying the bustle and the puddles.

I gave him the street and the number, opening the slider pointedly, then moving it shut again. But he saw me, Conservative voter that he undoubtedly was, as a wounded old soldier, and I could do no wrong.

I watched the grey masses, borne along by the same wind and rain as the car, subject to the same capricious laws as I was. I began to warm to their awful sameness, their dour British low profiles.

But these were the helmeted starvelings who had roamed the length and breadth of Ireland with fire and sword, reign after reign. The blunt instruments that Riley had had to rely on at Smerwick.

I drew the blind down, and closed my eyes. I got here, and I paid the ostler and groom, and I had the horses put to graze, and I came upstairs.

Under these rafters I took my quill, and I set more down. More prose. More thoughts and adventures, rimming the glass with a creamy foam.

But I kept the verses locked up in their box. A fragment no longer suitable, no longer able to cope.

The pills, Liz. The pills. I feel faint.

26

June came, it was cooler. I walked over lawns needing the mower, through clover and plantains. The baby was due, ten days now, and you were ready. A little testier, a little more forgetful.

But the days moved slowly. I took the weight off you, whenever I could, which wasn't often. I had the tables laid by Sheenane, with the spoons in all the wrong places. I let Harland go upstairs for your sewing, and your books.

But you needed movement still. You were raging against the little body in your crutch, whose rhythm was different from yours, and tired you.

When you were walking, and might have coped with it stirring, it lay still. When you were prepared to sleep, raised up on four pillows, it kicked like a maniac, and kept you awake.

So you grew more irritable, and altered your hours. I would go to bed and hear you up late at the piano, stabbing out those Clementi sonatinas with your long fingers.

Often I fell asleep alone, listening to the distant music spiralling through the floor from below, like a savoury eddy of smoke, the promise of a meal I was then too weary to go down and share.

When I got up early, you would still be dozing, restless in a bad dream sometimes, or waking with a sudden jerk, staring at me in irrational fear.

I accepted this. It had to be so. I was full of admiration

for your power to cook and to decorate, to darn a sock or to knit a toy bear, exactly as you had always done.

You would even have gone up the scaffolding, and scraped walls bare for painting, if I had let you. You were full of furious combative energy.

I saw your shifts of mood, and your occasional isolation, as the natural price to pay for our child. I often thought they were functions of my own changes, too, and the changes in the country.

It wasn't the baby that was creating the growing sense of menace. The baby was only the background.

We were coping with what was happening inside your body, and our reactions were clear, and understood. What was happening out in the fields, and beyond the trees, was another matter.

I saw a man with a scythe one day, slicing the grass down in long smooth swathes. He had his jacket off, over a fence, and his sleeves rolled up above raw elbows.

It was one of the Desmonds, for sure. I paused in my walk along the boundary between our properties, nodding curtly.

'Randy,' the man called, when he saw me.

Then he took his cap off, ironically. I thought. He was young, I saw, not more than sixteen.

'I'm Paul's boy,' he called again. 'Fine weather, Spencer.'

I walked on, seething. I wasn't Spencer to him, and he knew I wasn't. It was insolence, and it was meant to be. They were testing my temper.

There were other signs. Gates left unlocked, a forced pane in an outhouse window, chips in the stonework by a barn door where someone seemed to have thrown a stone. Minor irritations, goadings.

Nothing too serious, you might say. But I was prepared for trouble when Harland mentioned the break-in.

It was after five, and he was enjoying a cigarette while

165

he watched the bullocks grazing towards the woods. As always with Harland, you had the sense of another pair of eyes in the back of his head, knowing that you were coming.

At any rate, he turned in good time, and was reaching down to rub the fur under Hengist's chin, as I lurched up from the croquet lawn.

I was helping to walk Hengist's tea off, hoping he might select the meadow and not the gravel for his fertilizing deposits. They're good for grass, but they muck up shoes.

'It's getting long,' I said to Harland, nodding at the growth of green, and the buttercups.

But he didn't answer, not directly. He flicked something away with his nail, and let the big dog go.

Hengist ran up along the fence and squeezed through a gap into the meadow. I liked his weight and his awkwardness, and I sensed that Harland felt the same, phlegmatic though he always was about animals.

'Needs a brush,' Harland said, smoothing his palms. 'Get rid of those ticks in his hair.'

Hengist was racing for the wood, avoiding the bullocks by a wide margin. So far he'd given them no trouble. They were alien to him, they smelled funny.

'I'll mow tomorrow,' Harland was saying, and then there were clouds low over the trees, and then Hengist was out of sight, and then we heard the shot.

The rhododendrons were in full flower. Orange centres and purple surrounds. You could stand under any one of the ten bushes with a thousand plates of dessert going up on shelves at your back.

'Lie flat,' Harland had been saying, for years, it seemed, and I was down on my trouser zip in what was damp and hard.

My nose taking in whatever there was. Hawthorn, mint.

166

Harland was kneeling, click of the shotgun at my ear, the cold barrels along his cheek.

Fire, I found myself thinking. Kill the swine. Not one shall live.

But there was only silence. A thrush and a robin. A breath of wind rising.

I felt Harland's grip on my arm, followed his pointing finger. A man had come out of the wood, and was aiming with a shot-gun at a brace of pheasant moving fast and low towards the horizon.

But the birds were too far away. The man broke his gun, and waved to us. Then walked back into the wood.

'One of the Desmonds,' Harland said. 'Nothing much we can do, John. That loop of wood is theirs.'

Then I felt my liver turn over, and a sickness coming, and then a sense of cold relief. Hengist was trotting out of the wood, sniffing the cow-pats, and I realized that for twenty seconds I'd been absolutely certain the shot had killed him.

'Rather dangerous,' Harland was saying, voicing my fear, and perhaps his own, too. 'He had no right to be aiming so low.'

'But we don't have any proof.'

'I'm afraid not. He'd say he was firing into the air.'

I'd been shot at fairly often. Out on patrol with Tom Gray, and in Landrovers crossing the border, I was used to the imminence of projectiles bearing death.

But this was different. I didn't like the idea of not knowing what was going on. I had a queasy feeling, like someone walking over a trap. I didn't like the memory of that man who might have been only shooting pheasants, but probably wasn't.

Then I was aware of Harland helping me up to my feet, the shot-gun broken over his arm.

'I was meaning to tell you,' he said, a mite too casually.

167

'We ought to look over the sheds together, maybe tomorrow. A window was broken, and some wood taken.'

'Itinerants, Harland?'

'I don't know.'

But I felt he did know, and it wasn't itinerants. It was Desmonds again. The pressure was on, the first skirmishes in what might soon be a total war were starting.

'Let's go,' I said. 'We'll take a look now.'

So I limped with him past the leaking sewer, the coppice of new spruce where the gas was concealed, the back wall of the mortuary chapel.

It had started to rain, a light smirr on the thrush's nest in the hip of a pillar, the last dregs of the blackthorn we would soon milk sloe gin from, the dilapidated wall round the chicken run.

I turned up my collar. Harland had his keys out, and was fiddling with the lock. It came loose, and we went indoors, passing a heap of old furniture and a burst mattress, to where the wood was kept, the sound planks and splinters we kept for repairs.

Harland was pointing, and I looked up to where a pane of glass had been smashed, and a glazing bar split through. Room for a slender man to slither down.

'He must have had a cart or a car,' Harland was saying. 'He'll have thrown the wood out onto the grass and then climbed back and loaded up. There may have been two, of course. Quite a lot's been taken.'

I studied the signs of intrusion. Nothing too radical, nothing extreme. But a stranger had stood here within spitting distance of the main house, where you and I were sleeping unawares. It was threatening.

'I don't like it, Harland,' I said. 'It's the thin end of the wedge. It's got to stop.'

Some days it was Harland who was worried more than I was, but that day it was me. I don't know why. I had a premonition.

168

So that when we got to the next shed, and the rain was coming down heavier, and we stood looking in a splashing puddle, I think I already knew what we were going to find.

The sawn-through fastening, the padlock hanging loose. The valuable tools lying scattered about on the floor.

Harland's voice was very loud under the drumming sound of the rain on the roof.

'The chain-saw,' he said. 'It's gone.'

27

I went back with Harland through the rain and we checked in the main house to make sure no-one had taken the chain-saw across there and forgotten about it.

My hair was plastered over my head, and my heart was beating faster than it ought to already. But I stood alongside the high bench while Harland opened the cupboards and made sure.

No chain-saw. A can of oil and a broken chain, yes. The manual, stained with tea marks, and dog-eared, yes. But the machine itself had been ripped from its moorings and carried away.

You use a blade that can slice through a foot log in three seconds, you feel invulnerable. It's a power trip. Whoever stole or borrowed the chain-saw knew what he was doing.

'Someone's got a fallen tree to cut, maybe,' said Harland, fingering the jagged links of the old chain. 'It might come back.'

I shook my head.

'It's the nearest thing to a gun,' I said. 'They're trying to frighten us both. You take a chain-saw, it's like raiding an armoury for a rifle. An act of war.'

Harland switched on the light above the work-table, where the tool-chest lay open. He was a hard worker, but he never learned to put things away. It irritated me even now to see a hammer and a pair of pliers out of place. They ought to have been up on their hooks on the wall.

He thought I was going too far, I could see. He liked to have things done his own way, the same as with clearing-up. For some reason, he didn't see the theft of the chain-saw as too important.

I felt annoyed, and then I felt reassured. He might be right. It might be a borrowing.

So I leaned back on a tall stool, and began to breathe steadily. You get a rhythm in, it helps the heart. That's what they say.

'I'll feed the cats, lock the doors,' Harland suggested. 'Anything else, John.'

It was hardly a question, simply a politeness. Harland had everything under control. He knew what needed doing without being told.

I sat for a while on the stool after he'd gone, watching the rain trickle on the window above the moat. The moat, the water-tank, what you will. It surrounds the building on three sides, half-dry, half dank water.

On a still day you can hear rats plop, like fish, in the clogging weeds. There are bottles down there from before the Romans, before the Flood. Iron blades and equipment from former sieges. The detritus of battle and festival.

I listened to the rain, and I grew calmer, and I must have drifted into a sort of doze. But I wasn't ready when the shock came. I was simply awake suddenly, and Harland was there in front of me with the corpse of the Black Prince in his arms.

I wrote it several times. I tried to make it easier by coming in from the side, obliquely. But it doesn't work. It still makes me shiver, all over, when I think about it, the way it was. Goose-flesh, the skin of the dragon.

I used to be used to violence. Those men I knew shot to bits in the wars, blown up by mines in the streets. I grew a carapace over my pity. You had to. You didn't take the cigarette out of your mouth, writing deceased over their letters. That's what Philip said.

I know what he meant. I remember never waking for months without hearing the sirens. Walking to school

171

over shrapnel. Hearing the screams of the dying in the dressing stations.

But you get older. You grow softer. The sensitivity clarifies, the will loses its grip. I could mourn for a pet mole now, a nest of spiders.

I woke from my dream, I say, and there was Harland holding the black fur and bones in his arms, loose like a scarf.

'I found her beside the swing doors,' Harland said, softly. 'She was trying to reach her food.'

I put out my hand to the tangled, rusty-looking bundle, not realizing for a moment exactly what had happened.

'Be careful,' Harland warned me, relinquishing the body. 'There's a lot of blood.'

The cat's head lolled back on my hand, and I saw then what had happened. The coagulating red. The jagged wound in her throat.

Like a slash from a chain-saw. What else? But Harland, still cautious, had already guessed what I was thinking.

'There's new barbed wire,' he said. 'At the edge of the glebe field. She might have torn herself, and then made it worse, wrenching to get free.'

But I wasn't listening. I was out in the corridor, following the trail of blood. I looked down the long lane of flagstones, repeated in the mirror at the end. I saw the irregular flecks, and the footmarks going through them.

'She came in through the double doors,' Harland said, at my side. 'She must have been hungry. She must have thought she'd be better if she could eat. So she made for the food.'

I was by the swing doors, where the body had lain. A pool of blood, scratch marks on the wood.

'She was very wet,' I said, irrelevantly, noticing signs of rain on the stones.

Then I went back and lifted the body, and pressed the Black Prince's fur into my cheek, and that's all I remember for quite a while. Quite a while or the flicker of an eyelash, I don't know.

'You were out cold,' you told me, when I came to in the bedroom later, seeing your pale serious eyes bending over me, and beyond those the patterns of heraldry in the ceiling. Fabulous beasts and armour.

'He caught you as you were falling. It must have been shock. The double shock of the chain-saw and the cat.'

You were never as keen on the Black Prince as I was. You saw her as idle, and messy. But you knew how much the cat had meant to me.

I felt my paranoia returning, full force. Paranoia, no. It made sense. The two things were connected, they had to be.

'The swine,' I said, feeling my blood rising. 'They slit her throat with the chain-saw. They let her crawl back, to teach us a lesson.'

I looked out through the window. The rain had stopped, and it was a warm, peaceful evening. I could see a flock of sheep feeding on the near side of the lake. The hills in the distance were a gentle blur.

'I'll tell you this, Liz,' I told you, grasping your arm. 'I'll teach them a lesson for this they'll remember all their lives. By God, I will.'

But you were sceptical, as Harland had been. You stroked my cheek, and I felt the disbelief through your fingers. It made me angrier, and I sat up, furious.

'I mean it, Liz,' I said. 'You mark my words.'

Then I flung the duvet back, and put my legs on the floor, and felt sick suddenly, and was down on my knees. You helped me up from the rushes, the sweet aromatic herbs.

I lay amidst lavender and rosemary, and I grew well. But first I slept, and there was a dream of swords and burning, and in the end I became Lord Lieutenant of

Cork, and there was a feast, and fine women opening their legs before altars.

'The usual tangle,' I said, with a smile, when you brought me supper on a tray. 'Worry and violence, and its resolution by power and sex. You know my dreams.'

'You feel better.'

'I do, Liz. I feel much better.'

But anger had gone to be replaced by its distant cousin fear, and this I communicated more easily than rage. We ate our soup together, and drank our coffee, silence gathering slowly towards a need for a talk.

Under the hangings thick with dust, while ermine moths fluttered at the windows, I elaborated my thoughts.

'I exaggerate,' I said. 'I know I do. I jump to conclusions. The chain-saw's gone walk-about, we don't know why. The cat's bled to death from a cut in her throat. So far, so bad. So far, no further.'

'But it's only four days to the baby, give or take. We can't afford any accidents. We've got to keep calm, whatever happens. A scare is as bad as a threat.'

You had lit the candles, and the silver sconce balanced on a little table at my elbow.

'So what do you want to do,' you said, knowing I had a plan.

'I want to meet the Desmonds, and talk to them. I'll discuss the right of way. Try and reach some kind of accommodation. Or at least a truce, until after the baby.'

'You make it sound like a war.'

It is a war. A real war, I was thinking. But I didn't say this. Instead I poured you the last of the coffee, and kissed your eyes.

'I'm sorry,' I said. 'You know what I'm like.'

You didn't, of course. Not then, though you do now. No-one did, not even myself. The other self washed in and took me over, and then it washed away.

Sometimes I lived in the past, like a ship at anchor in a

174

foreign bay. Then I broke free, and sailed on the high seas, and found you, and I was safe.

'They'll be there at the Finnegans on Friday,' I said. 'I'll ring Jack and ask him to make sure. We can talk after the concert. I'll pick my time.'

You were in bed beside me then, but we didn't make love. You were too huge, you felt, and you couldn't move. You hated yourself, whatever I said to reassure you.

'I'm sorry,' you would say, desperately. 'It'll soon be over. I feel so guilty.'

'It doesn't matter,' I told you. 'All that matters is how you feel. You have to feel good about yourself.'

'I don't,' you said. 'I feel like a lump.'

'My beautiful lump.'

That was the night I woke later and found you on the floor. You'd slipped on the way to the lavatory, and fallen on your face. You must have cried out, and I would have heard your cry, and woken.

I knelt beside you, and felt your pulse. Cradled your shoulders in my arms, worried.

'I'm all right. I don't know why I fell.'

'The baby. Is it all right?'

You smiled, wanly.

'It's fine. It's kicking me. It didn't like falling.'

So we sat on the floor for a while, and you got your breath and your nerve back. I felt your heart steady, under my finger.

'Let's go to bed. I'm cold.'

So I helped you up, and we climbed in beside each other, and you were soon asleep like a child. I lay awake, on guard so it seemed.

Outside the wind had risen and was hissing at the corners of the house. The slate-ripping wind. The fringe of the hurricane.

It had been a day of threat, the first of many.

28

Jack Finnegan was the best Irish fiddler since Disraeli. That's what they said. I don't know why. It always seemed a funny way of putting it.

So far as report goes, Disraeli never heard an Irish fiddle in his life. I suppose they just meant Finnegan was the best for a hundred years. He was, too.

I mean you'd go a long way to hear better. It wasn't just technique. It was a kind of involvement, the way he'd treat the violin.

I remember something you said, watching the look on his face one night, with the fiddle cradled under his chin.

'It's like winding a child.'

The bow moved so gently, fingers touching skin. The sound came out like relief, like pleasure.

Jack Finnegan was over eighty. I'd met him once fishing, in the middle of the lake, on a dry day in February, and we'd spent an idle hour comparing notes on catches.

'That's my house, over there,' he'd said, indicating a roof and a belt of trees in the distance. 'Come round one night and we'll have a drink and some music. Finnegan, sir. That's my name. Jack Finnegan.'

Harland, silent in the bows, and then rowing, had been surprisingly deferential. In fact, he didn't even cock the shot-gun.

'Jack Finnegan was a soldier,' he said, as we glided back with a brace of trout. 'Then a smuggler. But he's very loyal to the Queen. They say he keeps a Union Jack in his attic. You'll be safe enough with Jack Finnegan.'

So we went round. Lodging the car in his drive, the horses frisky. Passing a troupe of chickens, and a raging Alsatian behind wire. Then across a lawn, and in through French windows overlooking the water.

'Ask him to play for you,' Harland advised. 'He's the best Irish fiddler since Disraeli.'

Jack Finnegan had a young wife. Younger, anyway. She greeted us in his parlour, a buxom forty-five year old with a face like apples and cream.

She had something out in a jug, poteen, for sure. But no questions were asked. I took a liberal glass, drank with care.

I needn't have worried. It was good stuff.

'Jack's upstairs. He'll be down soon. I'm Agnes.'

The poteen was good. So was the music, later on. So was the welcome. In fact, by the end of the evening, Jack Finnegan and his wife were our first real Irish friends.

We came away late, flooding the trees with light as we drove home, through tragedy and darkness. I felt the alien world of Ireland close in, as we nosed around the water.

But I didn't say this. You were happy, and I didn't want to spoil things. I kept my eyes on the road, waiting for the wire and the traps.

'They were very nice people,' you said.

'Very nice,' I agreed, and then, with a huge effort. 'We must see them again.'

So we did, more than once. We got into the habit, like several others, of dropping in for Jack's regular Fridays, when he made a custom of being at home.

Then I saw Paul Desmond there, and the times were stiffer, and I broke our habit. The Friday after the death of the Black Prince was our first visit for over a month.

We got there after nine, a close June evening with a lot of flies. They had the windows open, and there were people out on the grass, with incense burning.

177

The flies were a bother. You'd brought a riding crop, a rhinoceros-hide affair, and you swatted the air with it as we walked up the lane from the car.

'They're bad,' I said. 'Let's go indoors.'

But there was Jack, a vigorous gnome with a wild shock of white hair, kissing your hand, and leading us both to a table pitched on the grass, laden with nuts and meringues.

'You look Roman, Liz,' he was saying, tracing the contour of your belly in the air with an appreciative gesture. 'The mater familias in propria persona.'

He could get away with this nonsense. You reach eighty, people grant you some licence. A mite too much licence for my own taste, but where do you draw the line? Not on the wrong side of the best fiddler since Disraeli. That's for sure.

So I chewed my nuts, and I swallowed my resentment. You come to be mollifying, you can't always carry out your plans. But I had to try.

'Been playing, Jack?' I asked, sipping poteen.

He could sense my tension. He had the sensitivity of the very old, and the kindness of one artist for someone he saw as another.

'Not yet, John,' he answered, laying his firm hand on my wrist, soothing me. 'But I will, now you and Liz are here.'

You put your head on his shoulder, nice to him. Well, he was nice himself, he deserved your attention. Old he was, too old to be jealous of. But I still felt uneasy.

'So tell us about his book, Liz,' he was saying. 'Is he going to set this ancient land of ours in order for us? Show us the way through into harmony and riches?'

I hated this kind of thing. I've never got used to the jokes people feel they can make about what you're writing. It's almost a superstition. It seems to put a curse on the words. Perhaps it comes of not being a professional.

178

It was easy for Jack, so I thought. He could pick up his fiddle, and out the stuff came, like marmalade from a jar. Three pats, and a rush. But I had to sweat and plan.

'It's a wonderful book,' you told him, dead serious, helping the tension over. 'It's the best shot at setting things right there's been. It's a blow for Ireland, both the old and the new. But he won't say a word about it all before it's finished. So no jokes, please. And no questions.'

I remember the moment well. A fly on my cheek, another fly on my arm. You swatting furiously at the air. The precarious plate of nuts and meringues I was holding for both of us.

Virtuoso Jack, smiling but feeling crushed, the gnome with his foot in it. And a sudden sense of the heat, and the people closing in. Then the drawling voice, a voice I knew too well. Paul Desmond's.

'Now that seems a pity. A great pity, John. I'm sure we all have so many questions we'd like to ask. About your poem, of course, and what it's about. Really about, I mean.'

I felt my hands trembling. I put the plate of food down. Then I took a deep swallow of my drink.

'Ask away, Paul,' I said. 'I'll answer the best I can.'

'Well, that's very fair of you. Very fair indeed. You see, there are those who say that it's likely just to be propaganda. That you were an English intelligence officer with a bit of a literary talent, and you're sitting here, in your early and profitable retirement, whitewashing the past. And possibly blackmailing the future, into the bargain.'

Jack had gone. There were other guests, and he hadn't the time or the inclination to prise us apart. I took a breath, and put my arm round your waist.

'What do you mean, Paul?' I asked him, very quietly. 'How could a poem blackmail, as you put it, the future?'

I saw the twist of his lips, and the curve of his Guinness

179

belly, and I knew he had the answer coiled inside him like a tape spun off a reel. It wasn't his own answer, it was Hugh O'Neill's.

'By twisting people's arms,' he said. 'That's how you can do it, Spencer. By suggesting the Irish are ungovernable. By weaving a pretty story set in a country dominated by anarchy, where the only answer is English rules. English customs, English fucking boots on our faces. That's how a poem can blackmail the future. By offering false examples demanding repressive solutions.'

I don't suppose I was listening by then. I didn't hear the violin starting, or see the people streaming indoors.

'Listen to me, Desmond,' I said. 'I came here for a truce, but all you want is a war. You want me off my land, and you'll do anything to get me off.'

He looked shaken for a moment.

'You're paranoid,' he said, as if surprised. 'I give you my opinion about your poem – what many people are saying – and all you can think about is your land. You don't listen, that's your trouble.'

There were just the three of us on the lawn by then. Jack was in full flight, and the night was dark with the eerie majesty of his music. I felt your fingers tense on my arm.

'Let's go, John,' you said, whispering. 'I've got a funny pain.'

But I didn't hear you, not at first. I had the blade in my hand, and the enemy stepping back, wounded in the shoulder. A touch, a touch.

'I'm listening now,' I said. 'Oh, yes. And what I hear is the voice of a damned scoundrel who drives his bullocks wild into my yard. Who frightens the life nearly out of my wife. Who breaks into my sheds and steals my chain-saw and slaughters my cat. Who tried to terrify me and force me to leave. Well, you won't succeed, you and your

180

brainless, cruel family. By God, you'll never succeed. I'm here, and I'm here to stay.'

I must have been half-way through all this when you started to speak. You told me later, you had to repeat yourself two or three times before I heard.

'The waters have broken. I'm sure the waters have broken.'

Then I did hear, and I came up like a diver from a long plunge, and I went indoors and through the hall to the telephone, and I got the number somehow, out of my brain or a telephone directory, I don't remember, and I rang and rang and rang, milking the cord like an udder until they answered.

'No,' I said. 'Don't send an ambulance. I'm on my way. I'll be there in under an hour.'

When I came out, you weren't there. I tried to run, stumbling, fell on my face in the gravel. Then I got up, someone helping me, Jack's wife perhaps, I'm not sure, and I brushed myself, and walked on, fast as I could safely, to the car.

You were in the front seat, your hands on your belly, very tense and in pain.

'Contractions,' you said. 'I'm sure. They're coming very fast.'

'How fast? Have you timed them?'

'I don't know. No. You time them, there's one now.'

Your face puckered up, as with intense constipation, and I laced my fingers into yours. It seemed to last a long time, your nails driving into my palm. Then you relaxed, and I held my eyes tight on my watch.

'Drive,' you whispered. 'We have to get there.'

I had the lights on, the engine purring. Then your face puckered again, and I counted the minutes.

'Three minutes,' I said, frightened. 'There's plenty of time.'

181

But I didn't think there was. It was a long drive, and there might be trees down, or diversions. There often were.

'Keep calm,' I said. 'We'll soon be there.'

29

We weren't, though. It was a long hour. I don't remember much about the first part, except the empty road, and the green of the speedometer, with the needle up in the sixties.

Then you told me to stop, and you got out and climbed into the back, where I could see you lying sideways, your face in the rear view mirror.

'It ought to be easier in the back,' you said, and I said nothing, then I said,

'Let's try it for a while.'

I started the car again, and we drove on. But I didn't like not having you beside me. I told myself it was necessary, if you said it was. But I felt lonely, selfishly lonely.

When another contraction came, I reached my left hand round, and tried to hold your arm. I was groping, though, and it felt harder to steer.

I sensed the climax of the pain, and I thought I ought to say something reassuring. I schooled my voice to be calm.

'It's all right,' I said.

It wasn't all right, of course. It was painful, and frightening. But I couldn't think of what else to say.

I drove through a small garrison town, the broad main street like a square, gaping in silence. There were cars drawn up to a kerb. Folk in an inn, for sure, drinking behind those boarded windows.

I tried to put what I had to say into words, wasn't sure how.

'Liz,' I said, over my shoulder. 'I'm worried when I can't see you. Would you try the front again?'

'All right,' you said, whispering. 'Whatever you say.'

So I stopped the car, beyond the old control zone, at the edge of a conifer wood. I kept the engine running.

You opened the door and came round the front, hands at your middle, bent double. I felt a kind of impotence, an impossible pity.

I reached over and released the catch and pushed the door open beside me, and you eased yourself in, like someone carrying a bomb. I kissed you, and then I closed the door, and started the car.

I felt better now, more in control. There was no traffic, and the speed rose fast. I had full beam on, a great lane of light all the way ahead. It seemed like a symbol, an allegory of the future.

'That one was easier,' you said, smiling.

I hadn't even noticed you tense. I relaxed, smiling back.

'I expect they vary,' I said.

I glanced at the time on the car clock. Nearly a quarter past eleven. We'd been on the road for only fifteen minutes. I found it hard to believe.

The first car passed us in the other direction, a Renault. You notice funny things. There were women in it, four women. A nun driving.

Holy Mary, mother of God. Make it an easy birth. I realized that my hands were sweating, gripping the wheel like the rungs on an iron ladder, a thousand feet above the ground. It felt like that.

Then you were moving in the seat next to me, and I glanced over, watching your face twisting, the ecstasy of extremes. I didn't know what to do.

'We'll soon be there,' I said, irrelevantly, and lying.

But you were smiling again, the contraction over, another survived.

'That was a bad one,' you said. 'The worst yet.'

184

Then you made a great effort it seemed, and squeezed my hand, and leaned over against me.

'I think I'll have an epidural,' you said. 'Now I know what it's like.'

We were passing a castle, ruins of someone's protection. Face of a cow through barbed wire. The Irish night in all its peace and terror.

I wasn't reassured by what you said. You were having a bad time, and we had forty minutes or more to go. I let the speed increase, but I had to be careful.

'I'm trying to combine maximum speed with total security,' I said, with a sort of laugh.

I had to show I was trying. That's what I felt. It's my baby, too. I want to share in the pain. Somehow, the best I can.

Then there was silence for a while. Woods and villages. People occasionally, in a street. An old man with a stick and a dog. Some kind of mongrel.

'Not far,' I said. 'We'll be there before twelve. How far apart are they, the pains?'

But you were absorbed in holding on. You didn't know. I saw you shake your head, and I felt a wave of guilt for expecting science from you. I patted your wrist, a useless gentleness.

'I'm sorry,' I said. 'I'll count for you. Say when the next one starts.'

But I could see when it started. I fixed my eyes on the hands of the clock, and they moved in their cage, slower than I could have supposed was possible. Then I heard you gasp, and I knew the next contraction, and a bad one, was beginning.

'Two minutes,' I said, feeling worried, and not wanting to show I was.

But you weren't interested. You were fighting the pain, then gathering all your strength for the next attack.

185

'You mustn't worry,' you said. 'They're not all as bad as that one. They vary a lot.'

So it went on. The banal remarks, the futile efforts to put each other at ease. The sense of time running out, and the car too far away.

'If it comes too soon,' you said once, then stopped. 'Let's think what we'd better do. Go to the nearest house, I suppose.'

But I didn't want to face up to that. Some drunk stranger, half-asleep in his shirt sleeves. Not speaking English, maybe. Remembering the massacres, and the famine.

'Don't worry,' I said. 'We'll be there in time.'

Twenty minutes away, in theory. Then a diversion, the orange signs moving us down a side road. Hawthorn brushing the wings.

The road was winding, and I had to slow. I didn't know what might appear around a corner. Even at that hour of the night, you get sheep sometimes, even tractors.

'You're not sick, are you?'

I was afraid of nausea, my own problem. Somehow it was hard to get out of my own skin, to feel how it might feel for someone else.

'No,' you said, smiling. 'I'm fine.'

You never had any trouble with nausea. I couldn't remember, felt stupid. Then I saw your face contract again, and I thought the pain would soon be hard for you to bear.

We passed a farm, another farm. A white barn in the full beam, a stack of hay. Then bungalows, a row of pillars and a pair of doors like a crematorium.

'Nearly there,' I said. 'We're coming into the town now.'

The asylum was up on our left, a long range of concrete. Some days you could see the madmen walking up and down this road, their hands behind their backs like Napoleon. Or Mary, if they were women.

I reached the crossroads, turned left at the T-junction. Another hospital on the right, but it wasn't ours. It's a town of hospitals, that one. You can feel the pressure of sickness always, like a rain cloud.

'I'll draw up in front of the door,' I said, organizing our arrival. 'Then I'll go in and tell them you're here. Leave you in the car.'

We were turning past the green, the open space in the middle of the town where they hold the horse fair. There were caravans round it now, nose at the kerb.

You nodded, holding your strength in. I could sense you getting ready for the long haul.

There were one or two cars in the main street, the slope down to McClarty's, where they serve the best whiskey in Ireland, some say. Straight from a secret still.

A couple of men in black, like crows, were lounging by the door. One spat, seeing the Jaguar pass, echo of that other spitting the night we arrived in Ireland, six months ago.

I drove past, loath to raise my fist, my hand in greeting. I took a right, against the traffic where there was none, and it was nearly midnight when I ran the car to a halt in front of the glass doors.

The Virgin Mary looked down at me, in all her plastic glory. But I hadn't time for speculations, Catholic or otherwise. I opened my door, speaking to you.

'Wait here, Liz. I won't be a moment.'

You had your hand on my arm, though.

'Get a wheel-chair,' you were saying, drawn with pain. 'I don't think I could walk upstairs.'

I passed three people smoking, in the little clutch of maroon sofas to the left. Reached the desk, and the glass partition.

187

'Spencer. John Spencer. I rang. My wife's in labour. Outside in the car. Could you ring maternity, please?'

It took an age, of course. The dull girl fiddling with the telephone. The endless ringing in some unseen ward. The lengthy conversation, punctuated with laughter.

'They're coming down.'

So I went outside, waved to you, walked over to the car. I opened my door, sat half in, telling you what was happening.

'They won't be long.'

I don't suppose they were, but it seemed they were. A starched nurse in a uniform like a white hussar's. A steel wheel-chair. A man to push, smelling of Guinness.

Then we were rolling over the gravel, the linoleum. The lift was coming. The shrine with its red candles lit by a switch stood winking beside us.

I took a deep breath, watching you smile at me.

30

We came out into a corridor. Serious nurses, heavy women walking to and fro in dressing-gowns. A sweep of doors named after saints.

The labour wards lay opposite the lift, a short roll past a giggling sister on the telephone. There were sinks and white coats everywhere. A permanent air of expectation.

'Take your clothes off.'

You sat on the edge of a bed, undressing, while the midwife watched you. A bony harridan with a nose like a cleaver. I felt embarrassed, as if about to take part in a sexual threesome.

I went over and stared out of the window. A stark row of houses, then the hills. Cars parked in the spaces marked for doctors only, as if for a quick getaway.

Another contraction was coming, and I looked over my shoulder, watching you deal with it while the midwife rummaged in your hold-all.

There are no privacies. You bring your wife in for a baby, they go through her clothes. I felt a sense of being in the wrong place at the wrong time.

The midwife – and she was a nun, I saw now – was holding out your silk night-dress. Appalled by it, I could feel her disgust.

This is what caused the trouble. This is what made him go for you, put you into this plight you're in. It's obscene, that's what it is.

But she didn't say so.

'Don't you have anything older, simpler? It's going to get wrecked, I'm afraid.'

You shook your head, anxious to help, unable to. They were all we had, your pretty things.

I began to take in the room. Grey and white. A flexible iron bed, able to arch and contract, roll away on wheels if it had to. A corpse-carrier, centuries old.

It must have lifted more than one body down to the mortuary room. Then a pipe in the wall, for gas, perhaps. A pain-killer. Baskets and towels, for blood. The paraphernalia of delivery.

You were in your night-dress now, lying back, with your eyes closed. The midwife had gone.

'See you later,' she'd said.

Instead, we had a nurse. Fat and blue. Little round spectacles. It was all starting to seem clinical and horrifying.

Events were moving faster, as if in a nightmare. I was there on a chair, watching it all.

The contractions were getting worse. I saw your face wrench into lines, premonitory of a terrible old age. The nurse went for your back, rubbing and lascivious.

That's how you feel. That's how a man feels. What can you do? It's all women. Professionals and women, and you're in the wings. An irrelevance, a spectator.

They brought a steel cylinder in, a torpedo on legs, and the blue nurse gave you a rubber cup.

'We'll give you some gas,' she said. 'It'll tide you over.'

Three gasps. A wheeze and a cough.

'Does it help?' I asked, anxious.

You smiled at me, a brave smile.

'It helps a bit,' you said. 'Not altogether.'

You were on your side now, gulping into the black rubber. The nurse was behind you, doing her best, I suppose. More than I was, I felt weaker than paper. Useless here.

190

Then we had Humpty-Dumpty, our broken shell commandant. He was still half-asleep, I could see. Rumpled in a fair-isle sweater. But no less threatening, with that scab on his bald head like a medal.

'I'll be in again in a few hours,' he said. 'You'll be better after the epidural.'

That's all he said. Four hundred guineas, I was thinking, and this is all you get. Old skull-face rolls out of bed for a few minutes, and then he's away back to his cards or his dreams.

The man for the epidural came in. He was dark and supercilious. A tray followed him in, choc-a-bloc with sinister ampules and syringes.

'I haven't had to lay one out for a while,' the nurse apologized. 'I hope I haven't forgotten anything.'

Sweet Jesus Christ, I thought. I hope not.

The anaesthetist smiled, an ironic smile.

'Don't worry,' he said. 'I'll tell you.'

Then it began to happen. It took a long time, and the pain was getting worse. The gas was too weak, or you'd used it all up. I don't know.

I remember the iodine on your back, a long mustard rectangle. The ampule at the mid point of your spine, hanging in place. Whenever the pain came, he took his hands away, and once he wiped the sweat from his brow.

'Keep still. Keep absolutely still.'

I did the same. I didn't move a muscle. I felt a superstition that if I shifted so much as an eyelid some sympathetic spell would be broken, and the needle might leave you paralysed.

It took a long time, and I lived through it, a little. I let the anaesthetist make jokes, and I even made some back. I tried to be perfect, the caring husband well in control of himself.

But I wasn't, Liz. I don't think I was.

191

'A writer, eh?' the man said, once. 'I expect I'll be reading all about myself in your next novel.'

He smirked, as if this was very funny.

'You never know,' I said, striving to keep him at ease. 'You'd better make sure you do it right.'

That made him laugh. That was really funny.

'How does it feel?' he asked, examining you critically.

You told him. There was a long conversation about the exact areas of pain you could still feel, and how much. It made me breathe easier. The stuff was working.

But then I thought about after-effects, and I started to wonder. That was the end of the first stage, with the dark man buttoning his tweeds.

'I'll come back,' he said. 'If you need me, that is. I can give you some more. But it's best to feel some pressure down below, when you start to push.'

It was hot in the ward, and I took my jacket off, rolling my sleeves up. I felt more part of it, that way, I didn't feel I could talk to you much. It seemed interfering. But I sat holding your hand, an impotent squeeze.

'It's like constipation,' you said, after a while. 'As if you need to do some very heavy business.'

I thought about the baby. Six pounds minimum. You ponder about it for long, you get a tremble in your own bowels.

I suppose an hour or two went by. I was very tired, missing the exact sense of time. We were quiet there, very quiet, it seemed to me. No clock or traffic noise.

It was almost like a sensory deprivation tank. The world of the epidural. Nothing much to see, no colour or light and shade. No scent or taste, only the remains of Jack Finnegan's nuts and meringues in my mouth. Nothing to feel, only the soft relaxation of your fingers.

'You can start to push soon,' the nurse said. 'I'll get the midwife. The baby's coming.'

I must have been dozing. I heard her say this through a

192

sort of blur. Then I was hard awake, smiling at you. A man to go into the jungle with. You bet.

The midwife was back in an apron, a butcher's wife. Drawing plastic gloves on. Helping a basket for rags out from under the bed with her foot.

Lay it on, I was thinking. Spare me nothing. I could only go through like an acolyte, a surbordinate helper.

You looked stronger now, ready. Back on the pillows, your night-dress rucked up to your waist. The midwife taking your temperature, your blood pressure.

There was something wrong with the machine. They had to get another nozzle in before it yielded a reading.

'Normal,' the midwife said, and then we were off.

Three twenty. The top of the morning, the bottom of the night. The child like a one-person infantry charge against a held position, to be taken only with a lot of bloodshed. I knew the score.

Could be an hour, the books had said. Or more. Depends on how hard the mother can push.

So I lay back in my chair, watching the rhythm, trying to pray. Or hope. Or feel lucky. A ghost in the baby's dream.

'We'll do it this way,' the midwife said. 'Three deep breaths to each contraction. Hold them as long as you can, then let them go, and push. Hard as you can. Let's try.'

The contraction came, and I knew it was just a pressure now, and not a pain. A force at your rectum.

I saw your face tense, grow red, and your hands press down at your sides. Then the breath came out, and you pushed, I knew you did, as hard as you could.

I was there, but I wasn't there. The midwife was doing the work. Two fingers, three fingers inside your bloody vagina, feeling for the skull.

'That's the way. Good girl. You're a topper. That's the girl. Good girl.'

193

It went on. Each time the contraction came, closer and closer, you drew in your breath, held it, and pushed. Once you let go too soon, and the rhythm was lost, and the midwife laughed, a relaxing moment. Then it began again, a focus, a concentration, two people working together to deliver the child.

'You're a topper. That's the girl. Very good. We're nearly there. One big push. Good girl.'

On and on. Minute by minute. The steady rhythm, the fingers holding you open.

'I'm going to make a small cut. Nothing to worry about. For the last few inches.'

Then we were off again. Old skull-face by her side now, looking more awake. Even managing a smile.

'He'll be born by twenty-to. Or she, of course.'

Three minutes to go. A long time, and now, between your open legs, from the side where I sat, I could see the head, a shallow dome flecked with hair and blood.

Then suddenly, it was out. A whole head, with a face, features and ears. And then, in the same instant almost, a slither, and a whole tiny body, arms and legs, red as the sun.

A slit up the middle. Huge, it seemed. Like a striped cushion between her legs.

'It's a girl,' I said, knowing you couldn't see her yet. 'She's a girl.'

Then they were cutting the cord, near to the navel. Shifting her up to her mother's arms. A miraculous crying baby. Noisy and moving.

I watched for the afterbirth. The twisting marble column of the cord, the great ox heart she'd been living on. The placenta.

Then I reached over and touched her cheek, our daughter's. Kissed you on the forehead, feeling exhausted. It was over.

194

But it wasn't, of course. It was just the beginning of that long anti-climax, the first minutes after a birth.

Not knowing what to do, not knowing what to say.

I held your hand again, and you fed the baby, and then she was weighed, and I was the father of a seven and a half pound daughter.

A nun came in with a paper, while we were admiring the child.

'Would you sign here?' she said, a request, not a question; although, this being Ireland, one couldn't be sure.

I read it through. I promise to pay. Etc. You default on the fees, they send the baby back, I suppose.

I began to feel the menace again. The sense of people-watching. I signed, hearing the pen scratch.

They were getting ready to wheel you away, to a ward. The baby swaddled into a blanket, rolled in a small clear tank, like a fish.

'I'd better go, Liz,' I said. 'I'll drive home and be back in the morning.'

I felt unwanted, neglected.

You smiled at me, wan and proud.

'I love you,' you said.

'Me, too. I mean, I love you, too.'

We both laughed, the last laugh we had for a long time.

I took the lift, swaying down to the ground floor. In the hall, a man was leaning forward on his knees, a shot-gun propped against his leg.

'Harland,' I said, surprised.

'I heard the news,' he said, smiling. 'Congratulations, John.'

'Thank you.'

'I got a lift over from Jack Finnegan. I thought you might welcome a driver on the road home. It's a danger-ous time to be out alone.'

I felt the sense of alarm and competence that always

195

seemed to exude from him, like the smell of tobacco from a smoker's pockets. It mingled with my own weariness, my distrust of nuns, my skin-shallow paranoia.

'Good man, Harland,' I said. 'It was thoughtful of you.'

Someone cannoned into me as we came through the swing doors, and I nearly fell. He didn't apologize, was gone before I could speak. I felt very tired suddenly, limped for the car.

'Liz is fine,' I said. 'They're both fine.'

He hadn't asked me, but I felt that he ought to know. Then I got the passenger door open, and collapsed onto the seat. I must have been sleeping before Harland started the engine.

31

It could seem a dream, the rest. It could seem I never woke in the car, and the flames began to crackle inside my head, while Harland was driving.

Yes, it could seem so. But it wasn't. The flames were real, when they came. I smelt the smoke, and I choked in the dry air. Who doesn't?

The first time I remembered, we were driving home from a holiday, years later, just the two of us, and the house was already burning. We came round a bend in the road, out of the trees, and the roof was falling in, the fire leaping.

But that was Rebecca or something, a book I'd read. The image of ruin after the end of the story.

I remember another story, the fireman up on the slates of Clouds, one half of his body scorched by the heat, the other frozen by the cold.

It seems like that so often now. Most of all in the mornings, when I wake early, before the dawn. One half of me dying away into the past, one half still struggling free towards the future.

Some days I don't know which is going to win. I can lie back and let the history take me, and then it's easy. I publish a book, and I die, and they learn the lessons.

But other days I see a new Ireland. It wasn't the way I said it was, where they're always out to get you. I make a mistake, I read the signs wrong. I did what the English have always done. I was prejudiced.

Well, I may have been prejudiced. I know. But there was a fire. That's for sure, and it changed everything.

I woke in the car, sniffing. I sensed burning even before my senses were alert, and then I took in where I was.

It was Harland lighting a cigarette. The scrape of the dashboard lighter had lifted me out of my doze.

'I'm sorry, Harland,' I said. 'I fell asleep.'

'You must be fagged out.'

He spoke kindly, and I realized how much I had to lean on in Harland, a mass of deep feeling as well as a knot of skills.

'I'm all right,' I said, feeling I ought to answer.

I felt uneasy with Harland at the wheel. It seemed that this gave him a kind of power over me I didn't like. I took a grip of my weariness, the captain on the bridge.

'There were no complications,' I said. 'Liz'll be home in four or five days, I imagine.'

I sensed Harland nodding in the darkness. He was a good driver, and I scarcely felt the car turn on the bends. But he was moving fast. I saw the needle well over sixty.

'The sooner the better, John,' Harland said. 'When she's well, of course. It could be a tricky time for us.'

The car had made sharp right hand arcs, and we were descending the slight hill into Creagh's Town, a ramshackle village with a central square, more of a long triangle, on a tilt.

Something was different from usual. A bonfire had been lit in the triangle, and the blaze was dying down as we passed. A handful of children, a ruddy glow on their faces, itinerants mostly, were dancing around the embers.

One of them plucked a pair of sticks from the fire and laid them along each other to form a cross. A pagan spell, or a greeting. Either, or both.

I waved, and the child, a boy it was, made signals as if to order us on. An air traffic controller, or a guard at a barricade.

'It's midsummer,' Harland was saying, as we swung away towards the church and the pub. 'You'll remember the bonfires, John.'

I did remember. Year after year, the sticks piled and the turf laid in the middle to serve as kindling. The children painting their faces, the victory of light against darkness. The pagan ritual preserved as a game.

But I'd forgotten the date. My daughter had been born on the twenty-first of June, and I realized with a shock, and then with a surge of pleasure, that she was the child of the solstice.

There were more bonfires, or the remains of them. Once I began to look, I could see them winking all round the moving car, a ring of celebratory fires in the night.

This was the trailer of flames, the first hint of an ordeal by fire that was still to come. I felt an obscure, gathering sense of disturbance under my rush of joy, and then I remembered what Harland had said before we came into Creagh's Town.

'A tricky time, Harland,' I repeated. 'You said this could be a tricky time for us. You mean with Liz away, in the hospital, I suppose.'

I couldn't see Harland's face, but I sensed a tightening of his muscles. Then he answered, but he was slow to.

'Well, yes, of course,' he said, then after a while, 'You see, John, I think they'll seize their opportunity. What with you being away, going to and fro to the hospital. They'll put the pressure on, one way or another.'

'You mean the Desmonds,' I said, spelling it out, for both of us.

I watched the speedometer reaching up to seventy now, he was racing us home. The green dials shone like the eyes of cats in a jungle.

'Not just the Desmonds,' Harland said. 'It's the Farmers' Union. They had a secret meeting in Mount Royal, I hear. O'Neill spoke, among others.'

199

I took this news like a blow to the stomach. I knew what it meant. We'd had it all before.

'Land agitation,' I said.

'I suppose.'

The weariness was a tree, a branching ivy growing out of my toe, up to my belly, over my shoulders now. I wanted to let it reach my neck and my face, put me to sleep. I shook myself, and it curled away. I could still think, a little.

'But where's the point?' I asked, a bitter landlord with no sense of history. 'I bought what I own. I'm a citizen like the rest of them.'

Then I thought of Riley, speaking to a few solicitors, a planner or two, smoothing my way.

'You're a foreigner, John,' said Harland. 'You know you are, in their eyes. You were digging ditches in Somerset when some of them were kings. That's their view.'

I saw the grave at the crossroads, where a suicide had been buried. The wind was rising, and the tall pine above it shook in a furious gust. Our headlamps cut by and into the road again, after the corner, and the hedgerows were all in a wild flurry.

'O'Neill's a lawless man,' Harland was saying. 'You have to know who you're dealing with. His ancestors were drovers, fighting for their stolen cattle, away to the brink of time. He enjoys trouble for its own sake. It's in his blood.'

In the blood of you all, I thought. In yours, too, Harland, although you're loyal to me, as your man, your master. Not for a policy from across the sea. It's a tribal thing, a pact of the heart.

So root them out. Let the trouble-makers be deported or executed, the land settled with gentlemen from Dorset and Kent. There is no other way. I swear.

The car shook, as Harland drove. It seemed to be lifted

200

sideways suddenly, like a flying slate. Then it righted itself, and we glided on.

'It's a wild night,' I said.

'A bit of a wind,' Harland agreed.

We were nearly back now. The schoolhouse had gone by on our left, and the gravel pits. The roads were empty, only our own lights boring into the last of the darkness.

Dawn would be here soon, with its dark fire. A red sky in the morning. But we were soldiers, not shepherds, picnicking by the sword in a foreign land. The weather was neither a burden nor a spell.

I could hear the howl of the gale above the low hiss of the engine, an expiring breath. We turned through the gates, the great stone stanchions like legs of elephants, imperial grandeur.

'I should have the shot-gun ready,' Harland said. 'I mean, just in case, John.'

So I humoured him, lifting the dead weight of the weapon over the seat-rest from the rear seat. I broke it open, feeling over the rounded ends of the shells.

We came over the bumps and through the tossing woods, rabbits dodging away from the wheels. It was eerie driving at this time, with the mooning faces of bullocks greeting us now and then from a fence.

The wind was high and hard now, on the open stretch towards the house. A muddle of sheep sheltering under an oak, and then the tarmac, and the steps.

I got out of the car, swaying in the wind. It was loud, a baying sound.

Harland was out now, too, directing a flashlight for me to open the door. Then we saw it. A jagged gash, a scar of blackness on the darkness.

'Level the gun, John,' said Harland. 'I'll go in first.'

He had taken the keys from me, was close to the grained mahogany, the unbroken panel of glass, the shattered pane. One whole side, a yard by a foot and a half, smashed in by massive force.

I splayed my legs, feeling unsteady, bracing myself against the gusts, the gun in my belly.

Then I was doused in light, the overhead bulb above the door naked under its cone. Harland was in the open doorway, beckoning.

I heard him above the wind, a reassuring shout.

'It's all right,' he said. 'There's no-one here.'

I went through the doorway, and past him. There it was, on the floor of the hall. The body of a swan, wing broken, its neck like a twisted question-mark in a pool of glass.

I shuddered.

'It's a big bird,' I said, in awe. 'It's unbelievable. To think of it thrown right through that window by the wind.'

'It wasn't,' Harland said, in a quiet voice. 'But they want you to think it was.'

I watched him lifting the corpse from the flagstones, running his finger down the velvety breast.

'There's no blood,' he said. 'It was dead when they broke the glass and slung it through.'

'But why?'

Harland shrugged, letting the body drop. I stooped and laid my hand on the feathery wing. It seemed vulnerable in its death, as white and ruined as the limbs of a girl.

'Board up the door, Harland,' I said. 'I'm tired. I need time to think.'

So I went upstairs to our bedroom, and flung myself as I was on our bed, and I lay for a long time on my own, thinking of Patrick Sarsfield, and the ten thousand soldiers who fled abroad after the siege of Limerick, and the wild geese they became in Irish legend, and the wild swans they would be when they nested again in the stolen castles they once owned.

O'Neill had sent me a sign, sure enough. A message written in the sort of language a poet would understand.

A poet and a soldier, yes. I was John Spencer now, safe in my own bed with my shot-gun, and watching the fires of midsummer glimmer through my arrow-slits along the horizon.

I still had a chance, before they came to get me.

32

We had sand-bags in the hall, shutters drawn across all the windows. The electric lights burned all the time, and we ate in a cold unending glare. It was war economy, the mechanics of siege.

O'Neill was everywhere. He had spoken on television, they wrote about him in newspapers. A crunch was coming. Everyone said it was.

The woman in Westminster had spoken. Riley had been released from prison, he was back in power. He phoned once, but the line went empty before I could hear any more than my name.

Sean phoned, he phoned twice. The first time he told me the good news. I'd been made a magistrate, the government wanted alliances, would I help them through? I said yes. But why was it Sean phoning? I never learned.

The second time he phoned, it was bad news. The Farmers' Union wanted my blood. I was down as a Quisling, a collaborator with the old regime. I'd be best to leave, before it was too late.

I suppose all this happened. I wasn't sure. I lived in a twilight region between my car and my bed, your little room in the hospital and the vast ocean of the television screen.

I was trying to make some sense of it all. My life and Ireland, my sense of doom and my new-born baby girl. I drove to see you, sharing your awful jelly and sausages, and then I went home alone, caught in a dragnet of dreams.

'We have to arm,' Harland warned me. 'They may come anytime.'

So we bought another shot-gun, and a box of shells while that was still possible, before the guards imposed a system of permits. We locked the doors, and we shared the day and the night in watches, taking turns, waiting for what we scarcely knew.

The radio was a blaze of alarms. The television broke, of course, or was cut off, and then the telephone lines were down, and we nailed bars across all the gates to keep any traffic out.

It made trouble getting through to the hospital, but we managed, I don't know how. It was all a dream. Terror and menace rising to a crescendo, where O'Neill would step through and sing an aria of final violence, backed up by the Desmonds.

But at last, you came home, folding our little Francesca, healthy and pink, in a blue harness around your neck. I carried her over the threshold, like a husband with a new bride.

I must have been ill. I know I felt ill. You looked at me critically when we stood side by side in the bedroom, the iron bar across the door and the curtains drawn.

'Is this necessary? Is it all so bad as it seems?'

I stroked my daughter's cheek, a perfect shell under a quilt of many colours.

'I don't know,' I said. 'I just don't know.'

Two days later they came.

33

You burn a house, you need luck. I saw it so often. Riley or someone – Tom Gray himself once – lighting the first match, the first bale of straw.

But it wouldn't catch, of course. A high wind in Mayo or a fleck of sleet in Armagh, it doesn't matter. Something, somewhere, would always blow the flame out.

Then they would come with petrol or paraffin. The clear liquid – like vodka, leaving no afterflavour – sluicing onto the carpets, the pretty furniture, the detritus of a life going up in smoke.

Laughter, and another match. The boys in their uniforms clapping hands against the cold. It had to be cold, I suppose. The right symbol for the iron imperial discipline.

A garage where there might be guns or a bomb. A thatched cottage that held a priest or a man on the run. It was all the same. A frozen arm, a fire in a room.

It was Tom Gray who suggested our name to me.

'The Blazers, eh John?'

So we hunted the north and the west, arson squads with a taste for the Guy Fawkes routine. A lesson for treason in a scorched nest.

I never thought I would see the process reversed. It had happened before, in the days of the landlords. But that was for spite, we said. A settling of local scores. As if our own holocaust was anything else.

As if our pleasure in heaping chairs up, and throwing the worn bedding on top, and setting the faggots in, was more than vengeance for a man who spat in the road. A man who told a dirty joke when our wives went through in their closed cars.

The war went to and fro, flame for flame, down the centuries and across the counties. A torch for a torch, a sack for a sack.

So I ought to have known when I saw the Desmonds coming, all three of them in an open car, winding along the road through the trees. A shotgun on the old man's lap, in the back.

I could see it all through the telescope I kept on the parapet in the solar. The naval one I had from Sir Richard Bingham. Leather mounts, and a flaw in the lens.

But I saw what I had to see, the twisted grins on their faces, the sense of silence. I ought to have known, but I didn't.

I went downstairs, found Harland motionless in the hall, under the antlers. He stood in a lane of sun, his boots uncannily bright.

'I'll see what they want,' I said. 'You never know. But start the car in the yard, make sure the engine's warm. Just in case.'

I went over to open the shutters, free the main door on its hinges.

Harland cleared his throat, uneasily. That spare smoker's cough, like a crow's nest loosening in a chimney.

'I wouldn't, John.'

But I had the key turning, the jamb moving.

'I know,' I said, and I may have been smiling a little, I think I was. 'They're here for blood, I know. Do nothing, they may go away. Open the door, there'll be trouble. But I have to try.'

I went out on the steps, hands empty. I stood in the shadow, though. The portico for a screen against whatever they had to hurl. Abuse, bullets.

The car had come to a stop about thirty yards away. No-one got out, or moved. Only the boy, Randy, in the passenger seat began to whistle. A rebel air, a tune to taunt me.

'You're on my land,' I called, from the shadow. 'Are you passing through? Or is it business?'

There was laughter from the car, the old man, I thought.

'It's Desmond land,' the man driving answered me. 'You know that, Spencer. This land was ours from away back.'

I sensed Harland at my shoulder, the shotgun on his arm. But I lost my temper. The fat swine was too much for me.

'You're a bloody liar, Paul,' I called, furious with him. 'I bought this land for good money. You know that well enough. It's mine, and I mean to keep it mine.'

'We'll see about that,' someone said, Randy, I think.

Then the old man got up in the back of the car, aiming at something, levelled the shotgun, and fired both barrels, high, but towards me. Thrum, thrum.

It was all in slow motion, like in a dream. The knotty fingers tightening on the triggers, the dark Os where the shells were coming from. The whinge of the shot scattering.

Then the bits chipping from the pillar, fragments of stone ripped from a moulding an inch from my brain.

You can see the marks now where the shot struck. There and a hundred other places. The length and breadth of Ireland. Wounds in a building where someone missed his aim.

'A pheasant, John. It went up from the cornice. One of ours, it was. I never saw you come out.'

The same story. The same or similar, here and there. The intended violence reduced to an accident. The victim got away with a flesh wound, or was buried out of sight in the wood.

I was indoors, though, before the damage. Harland saw

to that, hauling me through the door by my arm, re-bolting the big shutters.

'I'll get Liz down,' he said. 'It's time to go.'

I stared at him. You don't believe the worst, not always.

'We could make a fight,' I said. 'We have to.'

But Harland shook his head.

'Look,' he said, pointing through the window. 'There are two more cars. More coming, I'll bet.'

I saw the battered Ford, the ancient Range Rover, the broken down, armed retainers debouching onto my terrace. A dozen or fifteen already.

Harland was upstairs, calling for you. Hengist had his tongue out in the back hall, panting with excitement.

'Liz,' I shouted up the stairs. 'Where's the baby?'

Then I saw your drawn face, peering over the balustrade.

'In the dining-room. In her pram.'

'Get your things,' I called. 'I'll bring her out to the car.'

That was when I heard the crash. Like someone dropping a scaffolding tower. But it wasn't. It took me a second to know what it was.

They'd thrown something through the window into the dining-room. It was glass breaking I'd heard. Then more. Then more.

I flung the double mahogany doors open. I would have done, I should have done. But they were locked.

I fumbled for the key, couldn't find the right one on my ring.

'Harland,' I called. 'I need the key, the key to the dining-room.'

But he couldn't hear. He was out of earshot, helping you down to the car.

I took a step back, I ran at the doors. Once. Twice. There was crackling now, a sound I knew very well. The smell of smoke, then a trickle of it seeping under the lintel.

209

They wouldn't give.

I felt a sense of a script running out, the words I could never say being all that was offered to me.

I took a chair in my arms, a huge thing on castors. I don't know how I could lift it off the floor. Then I flung it with all my force at the double doors, and the lock smashed, and I ran forward and thrust them open.

It was always the same. The fire caught fast with the wind in the right direction. The great bales of straw soon set the curtains blazing. The panelling kindled, the floorboards gave way in a hail of sparks.

I remembered a house in Down. I coughed in the smoke, choking. But this was my own house. This was the casket that held the jewel. This was the room my baby was in.

Antlers of flame licked at me. I went in delicately, a man dodging a herd of bulls. Fighting through. But I couldn't breathe.

I went down on my knees gasping.

'Francescsa.'

But she couldn't hear. The roar of the flames was too loud, and I couldn't hear her crying. Couldn't see the pram for the smoke.

There's a poem of Southwell's, the burning babe. I saw her face in an aureole of flame, the little martyr.

Then a long scroll was in my hands, with words written in gold on black, and I hated the words, and I tore them up, and the pieces fluttered like ashes into the air.

'Do what you have to,' a voice said in my head.

I must have been on my feet again.

'I won't,' I answered the voice. 'I'll do what I can.'

Then I remember falling. Falling slowly, and a line from another poem. I don't know whose. *The majesty and burning of the child's death.*

But I caught the line, and I fell with it, as a fish falls

with the hook in its mouth. Towards the bottom. Towards whatever has to be borne.

Later I woke in the car, staring out at the sky. At the rain falling, the sun gone. I was in the back, and I couldn't move. Someone was driving, Harland I suppose.

I didn't know. I didn't care. I felt your hand on my face, and the pain of your touch.

'Lie still,' you were saying. 'Sleep. You have to sleep.'

I tried to speak, if only to apologize. But the words wouldn't come through my lips. There was only a burning feeling, a sear on the skin.

Later I woke again, and a boat was moving. I could see the same sky, and the same rain.

You were there beside me, I felt your hair on my cheek. That, and the burning.

I tried to speak again, but I still couldn't. The boat was moving, and I was going somewhere. That was all there was.

Later I woke in the bed here, and the sky was dark. I could hear the rain on the roof, still wringing its hands.

'I'm so sorry,' I said into the darkness. 'I did my best.'

Only no-one heard. I felt your warm body along my burning body, and I heard you breathing in a calm sleep, and I felt too tired even for the tears to come, and I fell asleep, not knowing or even caring.

There was too much pain.

34

I am Edmund Spenser writing this, and I know what happened. Whatever may have been said before is lies, or a fabrication of the enemy.

I lay in my bed with my lovely wife Elizabeth, the floor sweetened with bedstraw, and the breeze coming in through the arrowslits. I had taken my full delight of her, in the old fashion, and she was feeding the child.

I saw my daughter's little head at the nipple, taking suck, and her hair was golden, as mine had been as a child. I loved her then, as I love her now.

My man Harland, in whom I trust, was keeping watch, and the sheets of the poem, on which I had worked far into the night, lay under a stone on the writing-table. A new canto, and one I believe the best.

I tell you, we spoke little that morning, Liz and I, being in the third day of our state of siege, knowing the worst at hand, and unable to do much, save pray and hope.

There being a party of stout men, good loyal fellows, and Harland here to command them, I felt that we might resist for a while a stern assault, and even best them. But I feared for my own life in the battle.

It was me they wanted, sherrif as I was, foe of their aims as I had been, and am. But no matter, so that my wife Elizabeth and my child survived. I had had a good life, and would die easy.

'See to it, my dear, that the poem goes to London,' I told her, my help-mate and my love. 'That is, if I fall in the foray.'

'Which God forfend.'

'It lies, as do all things, in the hollow of his hand. You know this. But I am old, and can scarcely live long, whatever the outcome. Wherefore, do not grieve. Only accept the inevitable, and take care of our child and my work, as best you can.'

But she, as women will, would cry then, and we lay in each other's arms, fearful and yet happy, watching our baby Francesca, rocking in her wooden cradle on the floor.

Then Harland, entering, informed us that a number of men were approaching across the field, and in what appeared to be some military formation, bearing weapons and the implements for a siege, ladders and fire.

I went out upon the battlements with him, and took the glass he gave me. It was a fine morning, a little chill for the time of year, and I could admire the last leaves on the oak-trees, on the way to the lake.

'How many are we, Harland?' I asked him, knowing already the substance of his answer.

'Fifteen, sir, counting yourself.'

I could see, through the ground lens of our telescope – a nautical thing, and a present once from Sir Richard Bingham to me, a source of pride – some forty or fifty men in the approaching party, several in helmets, and with breast armour.

'We are out-numbered, Harland,' I said, 'and there is perhaps not much chance of relief, not soon. But we must lay on, and save what we can.'

So the battle was joined. Surrender being asked for, and refused, a round of musketfire was delivered, with little damage done. But mortars being brought, they began with more skill, to discharge missiles upon us, and wrought some havoc in the stonework.

Nevertheless for a time we were able to withstand these assaults, and returned the fire, apparently killing one assailant and wounding another, whom we observed bleeding from a shoulder-wound, and upon the grass, where a surgeon tended him.

I doubt not, save for our lack of powder, that we might have bested them, until relieved from Cork. But this was not to be.

'Restrict our fire, Harland,' I warned. 'Else shall we be taken too soon, and with no defence for our own, I mean in particular Elizabeth, and the child.'

Thereafter we gave not volley for volley, but only a scattering fire, one ball perhaps to their twenty. Which noting, as was bound to be the case, our antagonists advanced more closely, until their vanguard lay beneath our main windows, protected by their moving shields.

From the shelter of these, two men crept round the back of the house, and with pitchforks and tallow upended a blazing bundle of faggots into our cellarage where the kegs of wine soon caught and increased the flame.

Smoke in my nostrils advised me of what was to come, ere Harland gave me the dire message.

'I fear, sir, that the fire has too strong a hold. There is naught for it but retire, and seek flight with the horses. Your life, and that of Elizabeth and the baby, are forfeit if you stay. Never care for the men and me. What cover we can, we shall give you, then swear we were forced in your service. We shall be safe. Now go.'

There being no time for argument, and in mortal dread for my family, I did embrace the loyal fellow as I could, leaving my own sword for his final stand. Then I called on Elizabeth and her two serving-women, and ran to prepare the horses.

What happened then I know not, much as I have debated the matter with my conscience and the Lord. I heard my good wife scream, saw her huddle amidst our children, Sylvanus and Peregrine. But the hand-maid, in whose care the baby had been put, now stood before me with the suffocated corpse in her arms.

I write this under stinking straw, hiding in the mess of a saddler's cart, and on the road towards Dublin City and the sea to England. What will become of us I know not, but the child is lost.

35

Later, I woke in the night again, and the rain had stopped. It was dark still, but I felt you stir beside me, and something had changed.

'I can see your eyes,' you said softly. 'Your beautiful eyes.'

But my eyes were full of tears.

'Don't cry,' you said, reaching your hands to my face. 'It's all right. The best is still to come.'

'O Liz,' I said, as the tears fell. 'I tried. I tried.'

Then you told me, supporting me in your arms. But I think I knew, though I thought I was in a dream. I heard a cry in the darkness, felt the stir of the little body as it turned in its clothes.

'I told you before,' you said, as you stroked my scars. 'But you were raving. You wouldn't believe me. You said it was all your fault, right from the start.'

I began to feel what I knew was true, but I couldn't accept it yet. It was too soon, too special.

'You were right, in a way,' you told me, snuggling close, and I felt the hollows inside your hips with my wounded fingers. 'You were too wrapped up in the past, so full of guilt you couldn't see through to the future. It took you a while to see. It's your own life you have to live, not someone else's. However grand that other life may seem.'

'It took a child,' I said, holding your lips close to my lips.

But the pain was too great. I had to let go.

'It took the child, saving the child,' you told me.

Then you sat up in bed, and switched the lamp on, and sat looking down at me.

'You saved the child's life. When Harland found you, you had Francesca in your arms. You were on the floor of the hall, under the fleur-de-lys. You were so badly burned, you know. You still are.'

I didn't need your kindness to tell me the pain of the burns.

But I watched the swing of your heavy breasts, full as a cow's udder when you swung them to the baby's greedy lips. I watched your intent face on Francesca's feeding mouth, a face of love.

The future had spread its wings. There was nothing to stop the forward thrust of its power. Not even the myth burning itself to a cinder in my tissues. I could feel its end, even as it hurt me.

You looked up at me seriously from your mother's task.

'The house is gone, you know. It went up like paper, I don't know why. We could see the flames like a midsummer bonfire. Four miles away, there was nothing but flames. I'm sorry.'

You touched a sore place on my arm, and I winced.

'It doesn't matter,' I said, forcing a smile. 'It was just a castle in the air. Going back to Ireland, it was all part of the same thing. Living out another life. Someone else's, from long ago.'

You smiled.

'The Desmonds may have the land, you told me. But they won't have your house. They did their job too well.'

'Well enough.'

Then your face clouded, and you remembered something else I already knew, or guessed.

'The poem,' you said. 'I'm afraid the manuscripts went up in the fire. It was all we could do to save ourselves.'

217

I looked at the white room, the Japanese paper lantern white on the ceiling. A room to begin in.

'There are bits in my brain,' I told you. 'Enough to go on with, if I wanted to. But I need to write something else now. From a different standpoint, with a sense of the future. I'll try when I'm better, soon as I can.'

Francesca burped, and you turned her over to wind her, a new being I had never known before, a wiser, careful person who could manage a child, and I loved you more for this, and wanted you still.

'The lady's gone,' you told me, over your shoulder. 'I heard on the radio. We're back in another England, a fresh reign. A major change.'

I laughed.

'The Queen is dead, long live the King.'

But it felt strange to be back in the Court, where so many had schemed and risen, not knowing which ones would still be in power.

I thought of Riley, wondered if he would survive. But Riley would always survive. He was too old to change, and the state would always need its executioners.

You put the baby down in her cot, and came over to lie beside me, in this plain divan on the floor.

'We have nothing now,' I told you. 'Only ourselves.'

But you ran your long legs down over my scarred legs, and I loved the pain, even as it made me sweat.

Afterwards, we lay in each other's arms, and the rain began again, and it made us happy, listening to the patter of fruitful drops in the darkness, and behind them the quiet breathing of our daughter, asleep and safe.

Later you fell asleep, and then I fell asleep as well, knowing that in the morning I would rise and begin to tell this story a new way. Not as a poem in dozens and dozens, or even as a novel with a set structure, chapter following on exacting chapter.

I would write of a skin sloughed and a past forgiven. A guilt absolved and a future accepted.

I would do what I could to atone, by being myself, as best as I could. It seemed a fair bargain.

Of course, there would surely be ups and downs. Days when I might slip back in the skin of the old myth. Days when the burns would seem too much.

I wouldn't cure in a flash. There might be setbacks and contradictions. I couldn't be sure. I still can't.

There are times when the old story seems more vivid than the new one, the luxury of contentment in sinking into a pattern.

But at least I see the light at the end of the tunnel. I know where I'm going, or trying to go.

It's a long haul. It feels like a long story, however short it may seem. I may not even finish it ever, but I mean to try.

I mean to be me, before I die.

CHRONOLOGY: EDMUND SPENSER

1552	Born in London, perhaps in Cheapside.
1569	Goes up to Cambridge, studying classics. Friendly with Gabriel Harvey, a student of law.
1576	Takes his Master's degree, but gains no Fellowship.
1576–1579	Busy writing the *Shepherd's Calendar*. Travels in the north of England, where he meets and woos his first love, Rosalind.
1579	Rejected by Rosalind, he emerges in and around London, seeking forgetfulness and preferment. Makes friends with Sir Philip Sidney, then at the height of his fame and powers.
1580	Neglected by Sidney's patron Leicester, he travels to Ireland with Arthur, Lord Gray of Wilton, as the new governor's propaganda chief, or secretary. Is present at the ambuscade at Glenmalure and the massacre at Smerwick, which he later colours for posterity. Becomes a friend of Sir Walter Raleigh, first encountering him as leader of one of the armed bands executing the surrendered mercenaries.
1580–1584	Remains in Ireland after the resignation of Lord Gray, but enjoys no advance in his public career. Busies himself with the composition of his allegory, *The Faerie Queene*, designed to justify British policy beyond the Pale, and to intrigue the flattery-thirsty Elizabeth.
1584	Reads aloud from the early drafts of *The Faerie Queene* to a distinguished gathering near Dublin, including the Primate of Armagh, the Queen's solicitor, and the Vice-President of Munster.

1586	Is granted an estate of three thousand barren acres and a former castle of the Desmonds, as one of the Munster Undertakers, and thus becomes a neighbour of the now great magnate, Raleigh, with his twenty thousand acres near Cork and Waterford. Settles and litigates.
1589	Is visited by Raleigh at Kilcolman Castle, and reads the first three books of *The Faerie Queene*. Revises under Raleigh's enthusiastic direction, and travels to Court in England, where the new version of the poem is praised by Elizabeth.
1590	Basks in a widespread fame upon the publication of the first three books of *The Faerie Queene*, but receives no preferment or position in England. Remains at Kilcolman, extending the poem through several more books.
1594	Meets, woos and marries a local girl, Elizabeth. Composes a fine Epithalamium, extolling the joys of wedded bliss.
1598	Is appointed Sheriff of the County of Cork. Upon the outbreak of Hugh O'Neill's rebellion in Ulster, the allied and *soi-disant* Earl of Desmond rising in sympathy and to regain lost possessions, flees from Kilcolman Castle while it is sacked and burned. Loses a new-born child, which perishes in the flames.
1599	Escapes to London, where he dies, refusing twenty pieces of gold sent to him by the Earl of Essex, on the ground that he has no time left to spend them.
1599	Is buried in Westminster Abbey, universally praised as the greatest British poet of his time, even by the contemporaries of Shakespeare.
1600	Just misses the beginning of the seventeenth century, which will see the eclipse of his reputation with the rise of drama, and the triumph of the vernacular, but enjoys some posthumous attention after the publication of his prose apology, *A View of The Present State of Ireland*, which defends repression.